BIG BREAK

Dedicated to Orbin and Marsha Crouch, my amazing parents-in-love.
Thanks for raising your son (my husband) to be such a wonderful man of God.
You are a blessing to me, and I love you!

Big Break
Copyright © 2007 by G Studios, LLC

Requests for information should be addressed to:
Zonderkidz, *Grand Rapids, Michigan 49530*

Library of Congress Cataloging-in-Publication Data

Crouch, Cheryl, 1968-
    Big break / by Cheryl Crouch.
        p. cm. -- (Chosen Girls ; bk. 5)
    "G Studios."
    Summary: When Harmony decides to start a food pantry for the needy in Hopetown, and
an unscrupulous agent is pressuring the band members to sign a contract with her, Harmony thinks
it would be a good way for the Chosen Girls to make a lot of money that they could spend to help
others.
    ISBN-13: 978-0-310-71271-8 (softcover)
    ISBN-10: 0-310-71271-8 (softcover)
    [1. Bands (Music)--Fiction. 2. Christian life--Fiction. 3. Concert agents--Fiction.
4. Poverty--Fiction.] I. Title.
    PZ7.C8838Bi 2007
    [Fic]--dc22

                                                                        2007023151

Editor: Bruce Nuffer
Art direction and design: Sarah Molegraaf
Interior composition: Christine Orejuela-Winkelman and Melissa Elenbaas

Printed in the United States of America

07 08 09 10 11 12 • 7 6 5 4 3 2 1

BIG BREAK

By Cheryl Crouch

ZONDERVAN.com/
AUTHORTRACKER
follow your favorite authors

Concert at the Shelter

featuring

THE CHOSEN GIRLS

& KCH

Benefit Concert at Cleft of the Rock Shelter

* * * * * * * * * * * * * *

Sunday 7:30 p.m.

* * * * * * * * * * * * * *

Admission: $10 plus
a canned food item

I don't want to just
'make a difference'

I want to make the
world different!

L.A. BATTLE OF THE BANDS

YOUTH DIVISION

FRIDAY 8 A.M.–9 P.M.

FIRST-PLACE AWARD $5,000

Ways to Save the World

Set up a food pantry in Hopetown

send used eyeglasses to Third World countries

Pack care kits for victims of natural disasters

buy✳ ✳today

- ☑ purple beads
- ☑ blue beads
- ☑ silver bracelet latches
- ☑ pewter crosses

yummmm!!!

My Favorite Food

brownies
chocolate chip cookie
    M & Ms ✓
peanut butter cups
s'mores
anything chocolate

Cole Bake
Mrs. Cole Bake

So Cool!

Aaahhhhhhh!

Mrs. Harmony Baker

Mrs. Harmony Gomez Baker

<u>Someday</u> I'll own a purple motorcycle and wear a purple helmet and fly down the road and feel the wind whipping my hair around. And people will stare after me and say, "what was that?"

Cool frijoles!!!

If I was ever in one of those pagean things (never! But if I was...) where they ask what you'd to change the world if you could, I wonder what I'd s Try to get people to ado more children from arou the world, maybe, or get people to teach oth people to read, or make sure every child has a chance to go to schoo Muy bueno ideas.

No, maybe I'd say to help people in Third World countries f clean wate

Lyrics

java joint

I went ~~something~~ lookin' here and there
for the answers, searchin' everywhere
because I thought it was up to (me)
to make myself all that I could be.

I tried people, plans, and ~~places~~ agencies;
believed only what my eyes could see.
But now I am tryin' something new—
gonna put my faith and trust in you.

I put my trust in you, Jesus.
I put my trust in you.
Can't do this on **my** own.
I'm so glad I'm not alone
as I put my trust in you.

Your Word says trustin' **you** is great.
If I do, you can make my path straight.
I'm so tired of **wanderin'** round and round.
Won't **you** put my feet on solid ground

As I put my trust in you, Jesus.
I put my trust in you.

BACKSTAGE
PASS
BATTLE
OF THE
BANDS
LOS ANGELES
PERFORMER

Or food?
eople have to have food.
ut they have to have
water too. Or maybe
he whole world peace thing

. too many problems
the world. I'm NOT
oing to be able to
solve this today.
Thank goodness I don't
have a pageant
anytime soon.)

beans

java joint

coffee menu

- **mocha madness** •
cappacino with mocha

- **macho machiato** •
cappacino with caramel

- **shot in the dark** •
straight espresso shot

- **double shot in the dark** •
double espresso shot

- **frozen coffee** •
coffee blended with ice

- **far-out frappe** •
coffee/ice blend with whip

mmmm!

- **fro-zone** •
coffee popsicle

- **just chillin** •
cappacino chilled with cream

chapter • 1

...

Yesterday I stopped for a slushy at the Quik Shop. I was standing there watching it ooze into my cup when someone said, "Can I get my picture made with you?" I didn't realize she might be talking to me. "Please?" the voice asked.

I turned around, and a young girl smiled up at me and showed me her camera. She asked, "Aren't you Harmony from the Chosen Girls?"

I asked her name and stuff—like people always want my photo. Then I felt something cold and sticky on my hand. The frozen cherry cola had overflowed my cup and was glopping into the little drain underneath it.

That's what I get for trying to act cool. I licked the stuff off my hand and followed her to the counter, where the clerk snapped our picture.

Isn't that amazing? I mean, just when I'm doing something totally normal, I get reminded that I'm—well, kind of a rock star. Don't think I'm complaining. Oh, no. The fame thing is muy bueno.

But I get this feeling there's more to it, that our band hasn't made it big just so people will recognize me at the Quik Shop. Like maybe I'm famous for a reason—

•••

Thursday Afternoon

Trin burst into my room. "Harmony! Are you psyched or what?"

I jumped up and screamed, "I know! Only two days until ..." Then we both yelled, "Hopetown Battle of the Bands!" Trin broke into a dance and I did an air guitar solo and sang, "I can't wait to play my bass. Onstage, that's my favorite place. Oh, yeah!"

"You're crazy—both of you." My forever best friend, Mello, sat in her spot between throw pillows at the head of my bed.

My new best friend, Trin, tossed a plastic bag onto Mello's lap. "You're so right," she agreed. "That's why we need you, Mello. You keep us grounded." Trin watched Mello pull a pair of white pants out of the bag. "Plus you can sew," she added, tossing us one of her stunning movie-star smiles as she flounced across to my sister Julia's bed.

"What did you do this time?" Mello asked, inspecting the torn hem.

"My boots caught on them at our last concert," Trin answered. "Sorry. Can you fix it?"

Mello rolled her eyes. "You don't pay me enough for this, you know," she complained.

Trin looked shocked. "You get paid?"

Mello sighed. "Do you have a needle and thread, Harmony?"

"Somewhere," I answered, digging through my dresser drawers. I pulled out old hair clips, two markers, a rubber band, and some tape. "Just give me a minute." I added some smiley-face stickers and two candy wrappers to the pile.

Mello laughed. "What a mess. How can you find anything, Harmony? I should just go home and get my sewing kit. Save some time."

"Ouch!" I yelped, yanking my hand out of the drawer. "See?" I reached back in carefully and held up my prize. "You should have more faith in me. I found a needle."

"Thanks. Sorry you had to spill your blood for it. And how's *your* super suit?" she asked me, taking the needle from my hand. "I might as well solve everyone's problems at the same time."

"Mine's OK, I think," I said, digging for thread. "Ta-da! Look at this. It's even white. I'm organized in my own scary way." I handed the spool to Mello and crossed the room to my closet. I reached in and grabbed the white suit with the huge cross sewn on the front. I laid it on the end of my bed and looked it over. "Mine's fine. You did a great job on these, Mello. You're an amazing seamstress, or whatever it's called."

Mello blushed and stared hard at the needle as she poked it through the white pants. "Thanks. But all I did was put them together. You designed them."

"That was easy," I said. "I just tried to make them look like the ones in Lamont's music video." I stood there staring at the outfit, remembering the first time we watched the *You've Chosen Me* DVD. Mello's next-door neighbor Lamont had turned the three of us into superheroes, defeating evil monsters through special effects he created to help us enter a music-video contest.

"Hello?" Trin asked. "Harmony, you're totally zoned out. What are you thinking about?"

"My super suit. How cool it would be if it wasn't just a costume."

Mello groaned. "It's *not* just a costume. It's a symbol."

"It stands for God's power working through us," Trin added.

"I know, I know," I answered. "But don't you ever want to see it happen? In real life? You know, right versus wrong. Change the world. That kind of stuff."

"I do see it, Harmony," Mello insisted. "It's in our music— that's how we're changing the world."

I carried my outfit back to the closet and slipped the hanger onto the rod. I smoothed out the suit, then stepped back and closed the door. "I guess so," I agreed. "And Friday's a big day for that, huh? Loads of people will be there."

"I'm scared out of my mind about this Battle of the Bands," Mello admitted. "Why are you so psyched about it?"

"Like you said—that's how we're changing the world," I answered. "At least for now."

• • •

For Thursday's practice, I decided to surprise everyone by bringing our number one official snack: chocolate-covered pretzels mixed with peanuts. At the grocery store I grabbed the stuff and looked for the shortest line.

I found an express lane with only one woman checking out. Well, one woman, her two little kids, and a baby. I got in line behind them and smiled at the tiny girls who peeked at me from behind their mom. One of them turned away, but the chubby one smiled back without taking her thumb out of her mouth.

The mom had a hard time getting money out of the diaper bag because she was holding the baby. She moved him to her other arm and put the bag on the counter, digging through it with her right hand.

"I know there's more in here somewhere," she said, pausing to tuck a strand of long brown hair behind her ear. She pulled out wipes, a pacifier, and a stuffed animal. She turned her enormous blue eyes to me. "I'm sorry this is taking so long. I guess I shouldn't be in the express lane ..."

I told her it was fine, even though I did feel a little irritated. Because of her, I'd be late for practice at the shed. Couldn't she keep all her money in the outside pocket? How hard is that?

She started putting stuff back in her bag and said, "Um ... I won't get the bananas. Or the grapes. Sorry—"

The girl with her thumb in her mouth said, "'Nanas!"

Her mom said, "Maybe next time, sweetie."

The little girl whimpered. "I want 'nanas. *Pweese*, Mommy."

I looked at the other stuff moving down the conveyor belt toward the bags. Diapers, milk, eggs. Then I looked at the mom, whose eyes started to water and redden. "I said we'll try next time," she whispered to her daughter.

Oh. I finally got it. It wasn't that she couldn't *find* the money.

She didn't *have* the money. For bananas and grapes.

The checker guy set the fruit aside, and the woman paid for everything else. She moved her kids to the end of the counter and started putting stuff in bags.

I looked at the family, but suddenly I saw myself with Mamma and my sister and brother ten years ago. We'd just moved to the States from Peru, and my papi couldn't find work. The money they brought to live on was gone.

I had asked Mamma for bananas. "Yo quiero plátanos. Por favor, Mamma."

"Luego, mia mija," Mamma answered.

I felt the tears streaming down my face as I blinked away this vision of my own hungry childhood.

"Eight forty-two," the checker said in a loud voice. I blinked again and looked at him. He seemed irritated.

I whispered, "I'll take the bananas and grapes, please."

He shrugged and rang them up with my snack stuff.

I grabbed it all and ran to catch the mom. "Excuse me," I said, tugging on her sleeve.

She turned around. I said, "Um, I got those bananas. And the grapes — for your kids."

She stood up real tall and stuck her nose in the air. I could tell she wanted to say no.

I didn't give her a chance. "I know how it is — I'm kinda organizationally challenged too," I said with a laugh. "I've done that before, where I can't find my money. Please take it." I held the bag out. The little thumb-sucker reached for it. Her mom pulled her away.

"Maybe I'll see you in here again," I continued. "Then you can pay me back. After you find your money."

I watched the mom's blue eyes get all watery again, but this time she smiled. "Thanks," she said. "I'll look for you."

I practically ran to the garage in Mello's backyard where we used to play dolls and house when we were little. Now it's our studio—and a way cool place to hang. We call it the shed.

They were already warming up when I threw the door open. "I know what we can do!" I shouted.

Mello's drumsticks froze, and Trin's last guitar note hung in the air. Lamont looked up from the soundboard.

"We can feed hungry kids," I said. "Let's start a food pantry right here in Hopetown."

"And this idea came from ... where?" Trin asked.

"Does it matter?" I shot back. "There are kids in our town who can't eat decent food because their parents don't have enough money. *We* have money for fun stuff like, like ... chocolate-covered pretzels and peanuts." I held the bag up. "And we should help."

Trin put her guitar down and reached for the bag. I handed it to her. "So, are you in?" I asked.

"Starting a food pantry is a big deal," Mello said, grabbing an empty bowl and holding it out as Trin dumped out the pretzels and peanuts.

"Seriously," Lamont added. "You have to have a building and workers and ... food." He stuffed his mouth full and started chewing.

"We can get all that," I insisted.

Lamont flopped onto the old tan couch. "How?"

"With the money from Chosen Girls."

Mello shook her head. "It's not like we have unlimited funds, Harmony. If we start a food pantry, people need to be able to count on it. What if people got used to coming, and then we ran out of money and had to shut it down?"

"We'll just have to make sure that doesn't happen," I answered.

Trin said, "And your plan for doing that is . . . ?"

My phone rang the tune for Unknown.

I answered it, and a woman started talking so fast my brain could hardly keep up.

"This is Larinda Higgins. I'm a talent agent with the Shining Stars Agency out of New York City. I'm sure you've heard of us—we represent many of the biggest names in pop, rock, and country music today. I am speaking with Harmony Gomez, correct? And you are the manager for the Chosen Girls?"

I gulped but finally managed to say yes.

"Good!" she said. "I know a bright, talented, young band manager like yourself would of course be busy looking out for the best interests of your band. I'm sure you've spent hours researching talent agencies—"

"Well, actually—"

"No doubt that's how you know about Shining Stars. Maybe you were afraid to call a company as large and well-known as ours, Harmony. I can certainly understand why. The Chosen Girls are untried, really. A few concerts under your belts, a few contests, yes, but, frankly, nothing like the big names our company usually represents."

"Um, uh, OK . . . ," I stammered.

"Don't be offended, Harmony. Everyone has to start some-where. It's amazing you've accomplished what you have without an agent. It's a dog-eat-dog world out there. I'm sure you've discovered that by now. Am I right?"

I tried to think. "Well, yeah, I guess . . ."

"That's why I am thrilled to be the one to tell you this unbelievable news. Harmony, the Shining Stars Agency is interested in the Chosen Girls!"

My heart beat faster.

"I'm not prepared to offer you a contract, you understand," she continued. "But we have our eye on you. In fact, I will be at tomorrow's Battle of the Bands myself, to watch the Chosen Girls perform. Who knows? If I like what I see tomorrow, well, let's just say the sky is the limit for your little band."

The line went dead.

"Who was that?" Trin asked.

I jumped up and down and screamed. "That, *mis amigas*, was the answer we've been looking for. The hungry children of Hopetown can count on us—as long as we win the Battle of the Bands tomorrow."

chapter • 2

· · ·

The Battle of the Bands took place at Winston Park, where someone had been smart enough to erect a huge outdoor stage at the base of a natural amphitheater. It's a cool place to throw blankets or lawn chairs on the grass and listen to local bands every Thursday during lunch. But I'd never seen it so crowded backstage. Of course, I'd never been backstage at Winston.

"Harmony, can we go over the playlist one more time?" Mello asked. "I think I'd feel better."

I looked at our gear spread out on the grass under a large pecan tree, ready for us to haul it onstage any minute. "It's a little late now, Mello," I answered. "Only one band after this, and then we're on." I grabbed her arm and pulled her around toward the audience in front of the outdoor stage. "And right now it's KCH!"

I spotted Trin's pink hair close to the front of the crowd. I pushed people aside — dragging Mello behind me — until we reached her. Just then the announcer said, "Please welcome KCH!" and Karson, Cole, and Hunter ran onstage.

I cheered like a wild woman as they took their places, and got louder when Cole Baker played the opening notes on his electric. But when his aqua blue eyes looked straight at me and he smiled — cool frijoles! I totally flipped out.

They sounded great — and of course they looked beyond amazing. They're only the cutest guys at James Moore. In the middle of their second song Trin yelled, "They're racking up seriously high points for audience reaction. The crowd loves them."

I yelled back, "What's not to love?"

Mello said something, but I couldn't hear her over the music and screaming fans. I shrugged my shoulders.

She bent over and cupped her hands to her mouth like she might throw up. Then she started pushing her way out of the mob.

Okay, I knew what that meant. Stage fright!

I shot Trin a look and followed Mello, calling, "*Qué pasa?*"

When we got past the mob, Mello turned her sickly pale face to me. She held her stomach and said, "I have the playlist somewhere. I've got to find it. If I don't look at it I'll be sick. I don't want to mess up in front of this many people."

I threw my arm around her shoulder. "Mello, you know the playlist. We're only onstage thirty minutes, and that includes setup and teardown. But if it makes you feel better, we can talk through it."

She smiled. "It makes me feel better."

Makayla Simmons walked past, followed by her crew. She said, "Hey Harmonica, Melodious. Good luck."

Before I could say thanks, Makayla added, "You'll need lots of luck with your pitiful excuse for a band!"

I thought Mello would barf right then and there. I started to say something, but Mello shook her head. I clamped my mouth shut and fumed as Makayla and her group laughed and walked away.

Mello let go of her stomach and said, "Thanks for coming, Harmony. Sorry about missing KCH. You didn't have to follow me."

I gave her a quick hug. "You're more important than KCH. And I'm sure you wouldn't miss Karson on bass unless it was serious." As we started toward our equipment I asked, "But why are you so freaked, Mello? We've done this a hundred times."

"No, we haven't."

I waved my hands around. "Sure we have, Mello. A new stage, a different crowd maybe—is that what's bothering you?"

"No. This isn't a concert. It's a contest. Our first live competition. There are judges out there waiting to analyze everything about us, from our costumes to our lyrics. And all these other bands—I didn't know so many people were this good."

"I'm with you on that," I agreed. "Some of these bands can rock. But don't blow it, Mello. We need this win."

We reached our stuff and Mello picked up her drumsticks. "Makayla's band sounded better than ever," she said, starting a roll on her snare. "I wish we didn't have to compete against them every time."

Trin and Lamont joined us. Lamont said, "Competition from the Snob Mob? Never. You women can blow them away any day. Are you ready?"

"Sí," I answered. "This is going to be way fun."

Trin strapped on her electric and said, "Let's rock, Chosen Girls."

I looked at Mello. She picked up a snare and grinned. "Definitely."

We set up fast so we'd have time to do all our songs. When everything was in place, and we were ready to start, I got this awful feeling. I didn't worry too much about the judges. But that agent from Shining Stars was in the audience somewhere.

Trin looked at me, then at Mello. We nodded.

I thought, *What if we bomb?*

So much can go wrong in a live performance. Broken guitar strings, a faulty sound system.

Mello tapped four beats.

What if the crowd hates us? That agent will drop us in nothing flat.

I came in on bass.

Then we won't be able to start that food pantry, and those little kids might not get more bananas for a long time.

So far we sounded decent.

Look at Makayla and her buddies strutting around behind the crowd, acting like they aren't paying attention.

Trin started singing "Top of the World."

Lamont said we could blow them away.

We sang the chorus.

Let's prove him right.

We did. At least it felt like it. The crowd was so *there*—so into our music. I forgot it was a contest and let myself slide into the music too. Twenty minutes flew by, and when we finished everyone screamed for more.

Trin said, "I *so* want to do an encore!"

Mello nodded. "Me too—but look at the timekeeper."

I looked at the guy in the front row. His sign read Four Minutes. If we didn't have our stuff totally off the stage by then, we'd be disqualified.

I held up my hands and smiled at the crowd. Trin pointed at her watch and shrugged. Then the three of us kind of bowed and started packing up. Lamont ran onstage to help us.

People kept cheering. They didn't stop until we got the last piece of equipment off the stage.

Very, very cool.

• • •

That night we met the guys at Java Joint to celebrate. Cole lifted his frozen mocha into the air. "Congratulations, Chosen Girls! First place!" he said with a smile. "That was your best performance yet."

Lamont raised his glass. "It all hinges on the soundman, you know," he bragged. "People think it's the singers or the guitars, when really . . ."

I laughed and said, "Be quiet, Lamont." The rest of us raised our glasses and clinked them together. "You rocked too," I told Cole. "Congrats on third."

"Definitely. I'm glad KCH made the top three, so we're all going on," Trin added.

Cole grinned. "You may not be so glad when we beat you in Los Angeles."

"I heard that contest is beyond huge," Hunter said. "It's gonna be awesome performing in it."

Mello shivered. "Or terrifying, depending on how you look at it."

The door to Java Joint swung open. "Don't look now, but the second-place band just walked in," I whispered. "What a drag that Makayla's group placed."

"They're a great band," Cole said.

I felt my jaw drop. "Cole, I can't believe you said that."

"Admit it, Harmony," he insisted. "Makayla and her little group of followers have some serious talent."

Trin nodded. "Serious talent *and* serious cash. I'm sure it doesn't hurt that her dad's company has unlimited funds to spend on them."

Cole laughed. "Wouldn't that be nice?" he asked. "Somebody should harness some of those funds for something worthwhile."

"Like feeding hungry kids," I said with a nod. "Unlimited funds ... that would be so awesome."

Karson checked his watch and then drained his glass. "We've got to go, guys. It's Cosmic Bowling night at Barry's. You coming, Lamont?"

Lamont said, "Sure," and stood up. "Catch you women later."

After we said good-bye, I pulled my phone from my purse and waved it in front of Trin and Mello. "Are you ready?"

"For what?" Trin asked.

"I'm going to call the agent," I answered.

"Huh?"

"Who?"

I rolled my eyes. "The woman from Shining Stars. Remember? She said if she liked us today, her agency might take us on."

Mello said, "Oh, yeah."

"We won the whole thing!" I continued. "Can't get much better than that." I scrolled down until I found her number. "There she is."

Mello grabbed my phone. She said, "No, Harmony. Please don't call."

"What?" I asked.

Mello hid my phone behind her back. "We don't need an agent, do we? I like our band the way it is."

"Trin," I begged, "please get the phone away from her so I can call."

"No, Harmony," Trin said, shaking her head. "I'm with Mello on this one. We don't need some hotshot from New York telling us what to do and when to do it."

"But what about the exposure a real agency could give us?" I asked, thinking of those hungry kids at the grocery store. Kids we could feed if we made enough money. "Don't you see? It's time to get our own unlimited funds flowing. We'll never get a big record label or national tour on our own."

Mello crossed her arms and said, "Hello? We can worry about that stuff after we finish high school. Who wants a big label or a national tour now?"

"Do you ever watch TV? Look at magazines? Listen to the radio?" I demanded. "Half the bands out there are younger than us."

"And where do they end up?" Trin asked. "Most of them will let fame go to their heads and end up throwing their lives away, I bet."

I reached for their hands. "Exactly! But not us. That's what I mean—that's why we should do this. We're not like other bands." I squeezed their hands, wishing they could catch my vision for all the good we could do. "We have so much potential, Chosen Girls. I'm doing my best as our band manager, but I don't know all the ins and outs of the business like that agent does."

Trin stared at her cappuccino. Mello looked out the window.

"I mean it, Trin, Mello. We need this agent to take us to the next level."

Trin rolled her eyes. "We have *so* been here before, Harmony," she answered. "I thought you were over the fame thing."

Fame? How could she think I just wanted to be famous? Trin and Mello knew I wanted to feed hungry people with the food pantry. Why didn't they trust my motives?

And how could they be content doing what we'd always done, when we had a chance to change the world?

I looked at my two best friends sitting across from me, and all at once I knew the answer. Trin and Mello had always had everything they needed—and most of what they wanted—handed to them. They didn't understand how it felt to go without because they'd never had to. They weren't like the kids in the store. They weren't like me.

I blinked back tears and blurted out, "Maybe you both need to stop thinking about what *you* want and start thinking of others. It's not all about you, you know. How can you be so selfish?"

Mello did the huffy puffy and looked at Trin. "Have you ever noticed if you don't do exactly what Harmony wants, you're suddenly selfish? Doesn't that seem a little ironic?"

Trin stood up. "Yeah—like maybe *she's* really the selfish one. Let's go."

She walked out and Mello followed her. I just sat there steaming over my double-chocolate mocha.

A voice startled me. "They just don't get it, do they?"

I looked up and found Makayla standing over me. She flipped her silvery-blonde hair and said, "Couldn't help but overhear. Sounds like your band is destined for ... nowhere."

Before I could protest, she slid into the seat across from me. "You want to do more, don't you, Harmony?"

I didn't want to agree. Not with Makayla.

"You could, you know," she continued. "You're seriously good on bass."

I almost choked.

Makayla smiled. "Look, I know we aren't exactly best friends. Maybe we don't see eye-to-eye on some things—"

"You could say that," I agreed.

"But we're more alike than different, really. We're both talented, and that's rare enough. But we've got something even more special: the drive to succeed. To reach for more." She turned around and looked toward the door Trin and Mello had just stalked out of. "Unfortunately, most people don't have that. They're content with the same-old, same-old."

I felt more and more nervous about how well Makayla seemed to know me. And it bothered me that she thought we were alike.

Her eyes burned into mine. "Am I right, Harmony? You'd like to do bigger things, wouldn't you?"

I nodded, slowly.

"It will never happen with the Chosen Girls."

I opened my mouth to contradict her, but she held her hand up to silence me. "It's not a slam, Harmony; it's a fact. You know it as well as I do."

"Your point is?" I asked.

"Join the Makayla Simmons band."

I laughed out loud.

Makayla looked up to the ceiling and took a deep breath. "This isn't easy for me, Harmony. Don't make it worse."

"You want two bass players?" I finally managed.

She shook her head. "Ella is moving back east. I need a bass. And you're the best in Hopetown, maybe even in L.A."

I bit my lip and tried to take in the compliment, the offer. I remembered Cole's comment — that someone should harness Makayla's unlimited funds and use them for a good cause.

Was I the someone?

"Our band is going to be huge, Harmony. I won't settle for less."

I looked into her hard, gray eyes. And I believed her.

"So what's it gonna be?" she asked. "You can stick with the Chosen Girls and watch it happen, or you can join us and help make it happen."

I thought of the mean things Mello and Trin had said just because I wanted our band to succeed and make a difference in the world. I heard myself blurt out, "It's crazy, Makayla. But that sounds like a great idea."

chapter • 3

...

As usual, everyone met at the skate park Saturday afternoon. I didn't think I'd tell them about Makayla's offer. What
was the point? I could never *really* leave the Chosen Girls.

But if I wanted to stay, I needed to make things right.
Maybe this was the time to apologize for my part in the big
fight at Java Joint. On the other hand, Trin and Mello *were*
being selfish. And *they* walked out on *me*. I decided to wait
and see if they would mention it.

They didn't. Everyone got their gear and acted like nothing
had happened between us. Fine. I just wanted to skate.

Trin and Lamont listened to their iPods, but not me. I love
the sound of wheels on cement—it's the sound of speed and
action. I put on my helmet and pads and started with the
smallest ramp. I got some good momentum going and made
it about halfway up, turned, and zoomed back down. Trin

followed right behind me, screaming the whole way. "Aaah! This is fu-u-u-n!"

Lamont, of course, had to prove his manliness by skating farther up the ramp on our left, crossing above us, and coasting down switch on our right. "Oh, yeah, La-marvelous is in the house," he crooned.

I rolled my eyes. "Lamont, we're outside."

"It's a figure of speech, Harmony."

I stopped and grabbed my board. "Where's Mello?"

"Where do you think?" Trin asked, pointing to the bleachers. "Sitting in the shade, watching."

I sighed and said, "At least she's not reading. Watching is almost participating." I turned to Trin. "So what do you think? Are you ready to go big?"

She smiled. "Let's do it."

"If only it were that easy with the band," I mumbled as we headed for the next ramp.

We spent the next thirty minutes or so working on indy grabs, holding the board and manualing, which is kind of like popping a wheelie. I tackled every obstacle and every new move like it was a roadblock between me and my goals for the Chosen Girls.

I had just completed my first ever ollie onto a curb when I heard Mello calling, "Water break! Come get a drink before you dehydrate." She stood in the bleachers, waving two bottles of water above her head.

"Water sounds way wonderful," Trin said, coasting toward the bleachers. Lamont and I followed her.

Lamont grabbed a bottle and grinned at me. "I've never seen you like that, Harmony. You ate up the cement today. Good skating."

I smiled. "Yeah, well. Maybe frustration creates inspiration."

Mello handed me a bottle and said, "Your phone rang while you were out there." After I took a sip, I checked my voice mail. One new message.

The agent's voice said, "Harmony. Larinda here. Shining Stars. Expected to hear from you before this. You do have my contact information, correct? Perhaps you lost it, and that's why you haven't called. Anyway, congratulations to your group on first place. If you are still interested in making Chosen Girls a household name, get some of your promotional materials to me ASAP."

I closed my phone and took another sip of water.

"Who called?" Trin asked.

"The Shining Stars agent," I answered. "She's mad because I haven't called her."

"Forget her, then," Mello said. "We don't need to hook up with some kind of drama queen."

I shook my head. "Not that kind of mad. She just doesn't understand why we would pass up an opportunity like this." I kicked at the ground. "Neither do I."

Trin said, "Lamont, you may want to go skate. This could get ugly."

I grabbed his arm. "No, wait, por favor. What do you think, Lamont? An agent from the Shining Stars Agency wants to sign us! But Trin doesn't want an agent. She's afraid we'll have to give up control of the band."

"Hey!" Trin interjected. "This is not a control issue. I happen to think the band is getting plenty of exposure without an agent."

I said, "Trin, with you *everything* is a control issue." Trin acted shocked, but I hurried on. "And of course Mello is afraid, like always. Afraid that the Chosen Girls will be a success and she'll have to do more concerts — maybe even a tour."

Mello crossed her arms. "You're acting hateful, Harmony! I'm happy with the band the way it is. That's called being content. Contentment and fear are not the same thing."

Lamont held his hand up in a signal of defeat. "No way am I stepping into the middle of this. It sounds to me like you all have issues. Trin's right — I should go skate." He put one foot on his board and got ready to push off.

"Before you go, ask Harmony why she's so set on an agent," Trin suggested. "I think you'll see she has her own set of issues."

Lamont said, "Why don't you ask her?"

"OK," Trin answered. "Harmony, why are —"

"I heard the first time," I snapped. "And it's not what you think. You're so sure I'm all about being famous, you won't give me a chance to say what I'm really all about."

"What's that, Harmony?" Mello asked.

"I think it's awful that kids right here in Hopetown are hungry." I felt my eyes fill up, and I had to stop to clear my throat. "I want to help. We're leaders. We have a platform. I think we *should* help."

Trin dropped to a seat. "Is that seriously what this is about?" she asked. "Hungry kids?"

I nodded.

"But you always wanted —"

"I wanted the band to be big so we could make a big difference," I explained. "I told you that."

Trin said, "No you didn't, Harmony. You just said we needed tours and labels. And I think you mentioned unlimited cash. But I'm sorry. I was wrong. I never should have said you were selfish."

Mello threw an arm around my shoulders. "Me either. Forgive me?"

I nodded. "Of course. If you'll let me call the agent."

"Wait a minute," Lamont said. "You want the Chosen Girls to make money so you can feed hungry kids?"

"Yeah. To open one of those food pantry places, where people can get free food," I explained.

"I don't have a problem with the food pantry," Mello said. "We just have to think of a way to fund it."

I raised my hand like I would in class. "I know!"

They looked at me. "I heard there's an agent that wants to sign our band. Her name is—"

Trin interrupted. "Maybe there's another way. Like, why don't we do a fund-raising concert?"

I shrugged. "That sounds sweet and all, but it would be a one-time deal. We'd make, what? A thousand or so? We need more than that. I don't think a concert is the answer. Maximum effort, minimal results."

Mello jumped up. "We've got that website we started last year to raise travel money. We still get orders for purses and necklaces. I bet if we pushed, we could get a lot more money from that. And since we aren't traveling right now, we could give it to the pantry."

"And the Battle of the Bands is coming up. If we win, we'll get major cash," Trin added.

"Yeah, maybe," I said with a sigh. "But if we sign with this Larinda woman, it won't be a few dollars here, a few dollars there. We'll be in the big time. We'll have a steady source of money to keep the food pantry going."

"What food pantry?" Cole asked, plopping down beside me. Hunter and Karson walked up behind him.

"The food pantry we want to start in Hopetown," I explained. "I want to use our prize money — and our visibility — to do something real that helps people."

"Sounds good," Cole said. "Tell us about it."

"We thought of it because there are people in town who can't afford good food for their kids," I told them.

Karson nodded. "Cool. I bet there are a lot of needy people here we don't even know about."

"Yeah," Hunter agreed. "Let us know if we can help."

Cole's blue eyes lit up. "What about a fund-raising concert?" he asked. "Both bands together: KCH and Chosen Girls." He smiled and added, "If you aren't embarrassed to be seen with the third-place band."

"Muy bueno!" I exclaimed. "A fund-raising concert. What a brilliant idea, Cole!"

Trin tilted her head. "But Harmony, you just said a concert —"

"Would be so much more fun with two bands," I finished. "So when's our first practice?"

chapter • 4

• • •

Sunday afternoon my big sister, Julia, drove me down a block of scary-looking houses and buildings for the third time.

"Why don't these people clean up their lawns?" she asked. "Look at the trash — and how does every home manage to have a broken-down car out front?"

"Don't be so judgmental, Julia," I answered. "Besides, they aren't lawns, exactly. There isn't any grass. Did that red paint say what I thought it said?"

"Quit reading the graffiti, Harmony. You're too young for those words. *I'm* too young for those words. Surely there's a better way to cover broken windows than with spray-painted plywood. Lock your door!"

"What?"

"Just lock it right now. We're passing those homeless men again. You're sure her office is here?"

"Oomph! Watch the potholes. It says sixteen twenty-eight West Cedar," I read from my phone. "Are *you* sure this is West Cedar? Maybe this is East Cedar. Or North Cedar. Or South Cedar. I can't imagine any of these being her office."

I felt my eyes fill up as we passed barefoot kids playing with a tin can. The house behind them looked abandoned, and I wanted to jump out of the car and give them candy right then. Poor little things.

Julia slammed on her brakes and the tires squealed. "Sixteen twenty-eight. There it is," she said, pointing to a tiny building that should have been white but had dulled to a brownish gray. Weeds and litter covered the small yard, and a broken sidewalk led to the front door.

"That can't be it. Where did you see a number?"

Julia pulled to the curb and pointed again. "Look at the window by the door. See that little piece of paper?"

I looked, and my heart sank. A torn piece of notebook paper had been taped to the window. Hand lettering read: 1628 West Cedar. Shining Stars Agency.

I grabbed my canvas bag and opened the car door. Julia opened hers too.

"Where are you going?" I asked.

"In with you."

"No, Julia," I begged. "I'm trying to show this woman I'm responsible and mature. Walking in with my older sister won't exactly help that image."

Julia reached for my arm. "Harmony, look at that place. Look at this neighborhood! I don't feel good about sending you in there alone."

"You're not sending me," I reminded her. "You drove me here, and I'm going in." I paused. "Have you forgotten? We used to live in 'this kind of neighborhood,' Julia."

She blinked. "That was a long time ago. I thought you were too young to remember."

"I remember. That's why I'm here. I want to help people who are having a hard time." I pointed behind me. "Those kids back there—they could have been us."

Julia squeezed my shoulder and looked into my eyes. "I'm proud of you, Harmony. I hope it works."

I nodded. "Me too. And, hey, if I don't come out after fifteen minutes, *then* come in after me."

"Sure," she agreed. "Or how about I come in if I hear any bloodcurdling screams?"

I laughed as I slammed the door and headed up the sidewalk, careful not to trip over the jagged pieces. At the door, I didn't know what to do. Should I just walk in? I decided to knock.

I heard movement inside, and the door swung open. A tiny lady with black hair in two-inch spikes stood staring at me. She grabbed my hand for a handshake that almost broke my fingers.

"Harmony!" she exclaimed. "I assume you brought the promotional materials. I had begun to think your little band was afraid of success. Some are, you know. They'd rather keep control of their schedules, even if it means they never do anything worthwhile." I followed her to a card table holding an open laptop and flanked by two folding chairs. An old blue couch stood against one wall.

"I know what you mean," I agreed. "I'm not—I mean we aren't—like that. About doing worthwhile stuff. I—I mean we—want to do something that matters." I glanced at the cracks in the plaster wall behind her and tried not to stare when a bug started its climb toward the ceiling.

I thought about turning and running back out to Julia. This was the big agency that represented all the top bands?

Larinda looked around, as if she just realized where she was. "Oh! This must look awful—my temporary quarters. Shining Stars asked me to come ahead and check out the talent here. I've been so busy I haven't even looked for my permanent office yet, and everything's in storage."

I let out a sigh of relief.

She clapped twice, and I jumped. "So are you ready for fame? Success? Wealth?"

I couldn't hide my excitement. "Our band is thinking of starting a food pantry in Hopetown! And I've been putting together a list of other causes we could support. It's over-whelming, isn't it? All the needs in the world?"

Larinda smiled a tight-lipped smile. "I see. So you're all on the same page, so to speak? The others are excited about the possibilities with Shining Stars?"

"Well, um, they're getting closer," I answered. "They don't know I'm here right now, exactly. I figured if you agree to sign us they'll be excited, though." I fidgeted with my collar and looked away from her intense gaze. "They probably just think it's too good to be true, you know?" I finished.

"Harmony, I'm going to give you an assignment," she said. "I want you to get the others onboard. I want them here, begging me to sign your band. I want them congratulating you for being the best band manager in the history of band managers—all because you discovered the Shining Stars Agency. Do you understand?"

I nodded.

"One more thing," she added. "You need to get first place at the L.A. Battle of the Bands. That's a huge contest.

Winning it will speed you a long way down the road to success."

I smiled at her. "We plan to win. We always win."

She smiled too. A big, genuine smile. "That's what I like to hear," she said. She pointed to my bag. "I'll review the items you brought me and get in touch. Do you have a portfolio?"

"A what?"

"A list of songs, concerts, sample lyrics—"

"Well, no," I admitted, pulling everything out and putting it on the wobbly card table. "I mean, I put in some lyrics and the flyers from our concerts. And there's our first DVD—"

"This is helpful," she said. "I can take what you've given me and put it in a stronger format. I'll spend that time on the Chosen Girls, Harmony, because I'm trusting you to convince them about Shining Stars." She walked back to the door. "I will need you to send some photos. I assume you have good-quality digital ones you can email me? Thanks so much for stopping by."

I took that as my signal to leave.

"Um, thanks," I mumbled as I walked out. I tripped over a bump in the sidewalk, but I didn't look back to see if she was watching.

Julia reached across and opened my car door. "Glad to see you made it out alive. How'd it go?" she asked as I slid in.

"Bueno, I think," I answered.

Julia patted my knee. "Listen, Harmony. I sat here and looked around, and I have to tell you I don't feel good about this. If this agency represents all the top bands, why can't they afford a better office?"

"These are just Larinda's temporary quarters," I explained. "They sent her ahead to check everything out. I'm sure her permanent office will be beyond classy."

"Or so she says."

"What?" I asked.

She shook her head and pulled away from the curb. "She could say anything, Harmony. Just be careful who you trust, OK?"

I crossed my arms and looked out the window. "I know what I'm doing," I insisted. "Shining Stars will be the best thing that ever happened to the Chosen Girls." I looked back at Larinda's beat-up office and said it again, just to convince myself. "I know what I'm doing."

• • •

That evening I met Trin, Mello, and Lamont at the shed to get ready for the next contest. After my meeting with Larinda, I felt more motivated than ever. We had to win, and we had to sign with Shining Stars. Not just for the food pantry, but for all the other hungry kids around the world. I wanted to show them a list I'd started on my laptop called, "Top Ten Ways the Chosen Girls Can Change the World."

But first things first.

"Let's win this thing!" I said, blasting out a low note on my bass. "Are you ready to rock L.A.?"

Mello started a serious beat, and Trin joined in with a guitar riff. We were off and running. It's cool how much fun we have in practices even after almost a year together.

We'd finished three tunes when Trin said, "We want to play a new song for you, Harmony. Mello and I started writing it. It's not finished yet, because we need your help. It's about making a difference."

"We want to dedicate it to you. As kind of an apology, maybe," Mello added. "Sorry we didn't trust your motives on the whole agent deal. It's not like you were trying to pull something on us."

I felt a twinge of guilt about my secret visit to Larinda's. Was it right to sneak around and then expect my friends to trust me?

I forgot my worries, though, when they started singing. Trin sang a cappella, and Mello came in later on harmony. They sounded great, and the words were powerful:

Well it's not in fashion to be passionate and proud
but I won't keep it on the down low
just to blend into the crowd.
The bigger sin is silence, not the courage to speak out.
Gotta find a way to hide
the fear inside
and pray away the doubt
Cuz I know that I have a difference to make
and as long as I try there can be no mistakes.
I'm walkin' the runway the real way, whatever it takes.

"I only love it!" I told them when they finished. "And I love that you wrote it for me. You're the best friends ever."

"How touching!" Lamont said, pretending to wipe away a tear.

"So should we add some instrumentals?" Mello asked, tapping out a rhythm.

"Let's do it. Maybe we could get it ready in time for our concert with KCH," Trin said. We messed around, experimenting with lyrics and notes for a while.

During break, Lamont asked me, "Hey, are you serious about this food pantry thing?"

"Sí," I answered. "I've looked in phone books and online. There are other services available in Hopetown, but no place for free groceries. It looks like if the needy people around here are going to get any help, it's up to us."

"OK," Lamont said. "I think we can do it. After Mello mentioned the Chosen Girls site, I checked it out. Did you know you're getting a thousand hits a day?"

"Ohwow, that's way fabulous!" Trin said.

"Remember all that stuff you made to raise money for the Russia trip? A lot of people are still ordering it," Lamont continued.

Mello asked, "So we've sold more purses and jewelry?"

Lamont nodded. "Yeah, and if you want the site to keep bringing in money, you women need to get busy. Unless you have a reserve I don't know about. Mello, start stitching purses. Harmony, start stringing necklaces. Trin, do—what do you do, exactly?"

Trin crossed her arms and said, "I've learned a thing or two, thank you. I can string and sew with the best of them."

Mello dug through some storage bins. She handed me my jewelry stuff and got her material out. I sighed and started on the first necklace.

"This was fun for, like, the first three hundred necklaces," I complained. "Too bad we can't hire factory workers somewhere to mass-produce this stuff."

"No doubt!" Mello agreed. "Then we could bring in some serious cash."

"In the meantime, do you think we're making enough to keep a food pantry going?" I asked Lamont.

He grabbed a paper and read from it. "We've got nine hundred and fourteen dollars in the bank right now, plus twenty-three orders for necklaces and seventeen for purses. So if the benefit show with KCH goes well, I think we've got a great start."

Mello's face glowed as she sat at her sewing machine, lined up her two pieces of cloth, and started sewing them together. "I'm getting psyched about this. It will be awesome, won't it, to know we're making a difference? That people will get to eat because of the Chosen Girls?"

"I'm with you," Trin agreed. "The pantry is a great idea, Harmony. Thanks for challenging us to think about someone else."

I could hardly believe I'd finally gotten them onboard. It seemed like the perfect time to mention Larinda. "It is awesome, isn't it? And the more famous our band gets, the more ability we'll have to help others. I've been thinking about that agent—"

"Me too. What if you asked her for a list of references?" Trin suggested. "I'd feel better if we talked to some other people who've worked with her."

I looked up from my necklace. "You don't get it, Trin," I told her. "She isn't trying to impress us. We're trying to impress her. She's the one with all the connections—we're the nobodies."

Trin shook her head. "If she wants to sign us, we must be somebody. It makes sense to know what we're getting into."

I clenched my teeth and tied on the necklace fastener. I thought Trin and Mello were on board, but they weren't. Not really.

So much for the song they wrote. They said they understood about making a difference, but would my friends ever really trust me?

chapter • 5

• • •

The next day, we piled into Cole's mom's conversion van and headed for a shelter he had heard about.

"Next time we give you a ride it will be in a shiny new Dodge Viper," Cole said as he pulled onto Center Street.

"Isn't that, like, the most expensive sports car out there? How are you going to afford that?" I asked.

He smiled and said, "With the money from first place in L.A."

Trin laughed. "So if KCH wins, you're all going in together on a KCH car?"

"Not a band car," Cole corrected. "It's going to be all mine. Karson and Hunter want me to have it."

Karson and Hunter said, "Yeah, right!" and "You wish!" at the same time.

"I hate to break it to you, Cole, but first place won't get you a Viper," Mello pointed out.

"Besides, *we're* going to win first," I said. "And *we're* going to give *our* money to the food pantry. How can you talk about fancy sports cars when we're on our way to a shelter, anyway?"

Cole put one hand over his heart. "Ouch. OK, OK, so the Viper might be a little selfish."

"And a little crowded," Lamont said. "We barely fit in this van."

Cole stopped at a light and looked at the street sign. "Oh, here's West Cedar. This is where we turn."

Trin looked out the window. "What cute little houses. I've never been on this side of Hopetown."

"So what are we going to do at the shelter, Cole?" I asked.

"Talk to whoever's in charge. Get their input on a place for the food pantry."

"Good thinking," Mello said. "They should know where to go."

"Ohwow," Trin interrupted. "The houses aren't so cute on this end of the street. That yellow one looks like it should be condemned. And is that an actual homeless person on the corner?"

"I wouldn't be surprised," Karson answered. "I've heard there are more and more homeless people around here."

Mello said, "Right in our town? Seriously? So while we're griping about wanting a newer or bigger house, there are people sleeping on the streets?"

"It kind of makes you want to be more thankful for what you've got, doesn't it?" I asked.

The neighborhood around us kept changing as the houses got smaller and older. The businesses looked junkier and yards were messier. Old people sat on broken-down couches on their front porches, and a group of little kids shot baskets into a hoop with no net.

We got quiet. I was especially quiet as we passed the Shining Stars office. Thankfully, no one even noticed the tiny sign in the window.

We pulled up to a stop sign, and four huge guys covered with tattoos, chains, and piercings walked toward the car. I could tell even Lamont and the KCH guys felt nervous. Cole pushed the automatic lock button, and I jumped at the loud *click*. As we pulled away he whispered, "I seriously didn't know Hopetown had any neighborhoods like — this."

"Yeah," Mello agreed. "I've lived in Hopetown all my life and never been, um, over here."

"Look!" Hunter said, pointing. "Isn't that the street the shelter is on? We're getting close."

The shelter surprised us. It looked like an old school or something, and it was in better shape than any building on the block. The sign out front read Cleft of the Rock Shelter.

We pushed a buzzer at the front door, and it was opened by a short, stocky man with black hair.

"Welcome," he said. "I'm Eugene Camillo, the shelter director. What can I do for you?"

Lamont said, "We need information, Mr. Camillo. We're interested in starting a food pantry in Hopetown. Do you think there might be a building available in the neighborhood?"

Mr. Camillo smiled. "I can do better than that. I've got a huge, empty room here in the shelter I'd love to see used as a food pantry. Follow me," he said, taking off down a long hall.

At the end, he opened a door and motioned for us to follow him in. He wasn't kidding — the room was big, with nothing in it but a few broken chairs and a couple of cardboard boxes. "Would this work?" he asked.

"Ohwow, this is way fabulous!" Trin said. "I can see it now—shelves and shelves full of canned green beans and corn and soup."

"And macaroni and cheese and ramen noodles," Karson added.

I twirled around in the center of the room. "And it's right here, where the people who need it are."

"You know what they say: location is everything," Hunter agreed.

Mr. Camillo said, "I'm glad to see your enthusiasm, but starting a food pantry is a big commitment. I run a pretty tight ship around here, not some fly-by-night operation." He looked us over. "Let's go to the cafeteria and talk about what you have in mind."

We followed him to a large room with white walls, gray tile floors, and rows of long tables and chairs.

"This looks like a school cafeteria," I said.

Mr. Camillo nodded as he took a seat. "That's what it used to be. When they built James Moore fifteen years ago, they left this old building empty. It sat unused for years. Meanwhile, the economy got worse. People lost their jobs and had a harder time finding new ones. Some of them ended up on the streets—right here in Hopetown!" He shook his head. "I couldn't stand it. People outside without a roof over their heads. This nice, big building sitting empty. I finally convinced the city to let me buy it and turn it into a shelter."

"You bought it?" Karson asked.

"Well, I spearheaded the committee. People all over Hopetown pitched in."

Hunter looked around. "What a great idea. I didn't even know it was here."

"Not many people do anymore," Mr. Camillo admitted. "Public relations is not one of my strong points. Still, when people are down and out they find us."

"So do you ever need help?" I asked.

Mr. Camillo laughed so hard he had to wipe his eyes. "Yes, yes. There's always more work to be done than people to do it. That's why I haven't started a food pantry. But there's such a need! When people leave here and start fresh, it would be great to give them some food to take. And some people don't need the shelter. They've got a home, but paying for it takes every penny they have. I'd love to help those people with food."

"And so would we," I said. We told him about the money we already had, and Cole explained about the concert.

"A concert is a great idea!" he said. "You could raise money for the pantry and help get word out about the shelter at the same time."

"Maybe we could have a table at the concert where people could sign up to volunteer," Trin suggested.

Mello said, "Definitely. And we could charge ten dollars plus a food item to get in. That would give us a great start on the pantry."

"Amazing!" Mr. Camillo said with a smile. "I'm impressed with your ideas." His gaze swept the cafeteria. "Would this room be big enough for the concert?"

"Great idea!" Lamont said. "That way people can see the shelter and find out where the food pantry is going to be."

"They'll know it's real, and not just some made-up thing," I added.

"If we could take out the tables and fill the whole room with chairs, I bet we could get almost a thousand in here," Hunter said.

"So we'll need more chairs for the concert, and we'll have to borrow a portable stage," Trin said, whipping out her PDA and starting to type.

"And shelves for the food pantry," I added.

Lamont said, "We'll need some serious publicity. Posters and radio spots. Maybe we could even get the news to cover the concert."

I sniffed the air. "What smells so good?"

Trin laughed. "Leave it to Harmony to sniff out the food no matter where we are."

Mr. Camillo smiled. "It's the chili we're serving for supper. Would you like to stay and help?"

"Sí!" I answered. "If I can have a bowl afterward."

Mello gasped. "Harmony! It's for homeless people!"

"It's fine," Mr. Camillo assured her. "We always feed our volunteers."

We went back to the big kitchen and scrubbed our hands before we pulled on rubber gloves. Then Mr. Camillo showed us where to stand behind the counter. I got to be in charge of tea and water. Mello took her place behind the corn bread and said, "This is excellent! I'm so excited that we get to feed hungry people, right here and now."

I whispered, "I'm proud of you, Mello. Usually you're nervous about meeting new people. Especially ... this kind of people."

She looked surprised. "Harmony! Are you worried?"

I swallowed. "Uh, no. I'm sure they'll all be ... nice."

I had to prove I wasn't nervous, so I smiled and talked to people as they came through the line. Joe came first. He had wavy, sandy-blond hair and looked like a businessman in his polo shirt and khakis. I never would have guessed he lived in a homeless shelter.

But Raydeen came after Joe. Her wild hair stuck out in twenty different directions, and her green eyes looked right past me as she said, "Oh, lookie, lookie. We got us a new friend here tonight. Hello, friend. Lookie, lookie." I asked if she wanted water or tea, and she said, "No lemonade?"

I said, "No lemonade."

She started bawling her head off! She screamed, "I want lemonade! Lookie, lookie, lemonade!" I didn't know what to do. The line backed up behind her and she didn't budge. Finally, I said, "How about if you take tea for now, and let me check on the lemonade after everyone is through the line?"

She stopped crying and looked up, her eyes looking some-where over my shoulder again. "Tea? I'll have tea, please," she said. I glanced at Mello and stifled a giggle as I handed Raydeen her glass.

That's kind of how it went. Some of the people I couldn't imagine being homeless, while others had obviously fought some tough battles in life.

It opened my eyes to a whole new world.

After I served a man named Samuel and he thanked me, I heard my cell phone go off.

The agent!

My heart pounded as I whipped out my phone. What did she think of all the stuff I had taken her? Did she have a con-tract drawn up?

Her text message said "Are all the Chosen Girls ready to sign? I'm still waiting on those high-res JPEGS."

Ack! The digital photos — I'd totally forgotten to send them. And no, we weren't all ready to sign. Two of my big assignments, and I hadn't accomplished either.

After that, I had a hard time concentrating. I wanted to leave and get the pictures right then, but of course I couldn't explain it to Trin and Mello. I kept mindlessly serving tea and caught snatches of Mello's conversations with different people. One especially pretty woman said something about her husband bringing her to the U.S. from the Philippines, then divorcing her. She kept talking about some captain who had saved her life.

During a lull in the line Mello asked, "Harmony, what's your deal? You aren't even being polite to these people."

I shrugged, not sure how to bring up the agent. "I don't know. This is cool and all, but it's ... what? Fifty people? I want to do something bigger, Mello. There are people all around the world who need our help. I've started this list, see? And I keep thinking about Larinda—"

"Who's Larinda? Is she one of the women at the shelter?"

"Argh!" I growled in frustration. I turned to the person in front of me. "Tea or water?"

chapter · 6

· · ·

As soon as I got home, I emailed Larinda my best JPEGS with concert pictures and images of our CD cover. I didn't mention that I couldn't convince the band members to sign. Surely if she decided to represent us, they'd get excited.

Wouldn't they?

· · ·

The next morning, I was sitting on my bed, working on the list, when her email popped up:

> Harmony,
>
> I reviewed the materials you gave me. While they are somewhat amateurish, I feel they reveal a certain quality that many bands lack. After serious consideration (as well as consultation with

others at Shining Stars), I am prepared to extend an offer:
Shining Stars is willing to represent the Chosen Girls.

Sincerely,

Larinda Higgins

"Cool frijoles!" I yelled. I switched to our favorite chat room
and typed in:

mello. trin. lamont. i have big news. r u there?

Lamont: *yeah. i m making a power point of yesterday's visit
2 the shelter 2 show at the concert.*

Trin: *ohwow, way fabulous. i m working on a little talk
about the food pantry.*

Mello: *i m almost finished with flyers/posters. can't wait 2
see what u think.*

Lamont: *harmony, how about u? what's the news?*

I got cold feet. Maybe it would be better to tell them about
Larinda's offer in person. But I had to write something. I
thought about my list and typed in:

*i just read that every eight seconds a child dies because
they don't have access 2 clean drinking water!*

Trin: *that's so sad. but what does it have 2 do with this
conversation?*

Me: *excuse me for caring about people in the world who
are dying.*

Mello: *i thought you cared about the hungry in hopetown.*

Me: *duh. who thought of the food pantry?*

Trin: *so maybe u didn't notice we're all working on it. we
still need your help.*

Me: *you have it.*

Mello: *good.*

Trin: *hey. r we still on for shopping today?*

Me: *sí*

The perfect solution! I could tell them about Larinda's offer in person while we shopped. This was it—I was fully armed. I could officially say Shining Stars wanted us. I couldn't wait to see their faces and hear them say what an awesome manager I was.

•••

We each found some seriously cool stuff for the concert at our favorite thrift store. Mello found something else too. "I'm getting this for Jasmine," she said, holding up a brightly colored floral scarf.

"For who?" I asked.

"Jasmine. At the shelter. The woman we ate lunch with," Mello said.

I shook my head.

"You sat right across from her, Harmony," Trin added. "She told us that amazing story about her and her little boys getting kicked out of their apartment after she lost her job."

I still didn't remember.

Trin stared at me like I had committed some kind of crime. "I can't believe it," she griped. "Didn't you pay any attention? She said they might have died if it wasn't for the captain."

"And who is this captain everyone keeps talking about?" I asked.

Mello threw her arms up. "Unbelievable! It's Mr. Camillo. He's a retired Navy captain. How did you miss that?"

"Sorry, Mello," I answered. "I guess I don't have your talent for making instant best friends."

Mello's jaw dropped open. "Right. Yeah. That's it. You've always wished you could be more outgoing like me. I give up." She hustled to the dressing rooms, and we followed her.

"OK. So maybe I thought we were feeding needy people, and that threw me off," I said. "I didn't expect you to pick out a scarf for one of the shelter residents. I didn't know we were dressing them too."

Mello pushed open a door to one of the changing rooms and stepped in. Before the door closed behind her she said, "Why can't we do both, Harmony? You're the one who's try-ing to save the whole world."

"You're right," I agreed. "And I have good news. We just may be able to do it all."

Trin disappeared into a stall but her voice rang out clearly. "Why do I have a bad feeling about this?"

I went into a stall and started changing. "It's nothing to feel bad about. It's something to celebrate. I got an email last night from Larinda!"

"Who?" Mello asked.

I stuffed my arms into the sleeves of a white denim jacket. "Larinda from Shining Stars. The agency said yes! They'll take us!"

"Take us where?" Trin asked.

I pulled a pleated skirt up over my leggings. "To the top. Where else?"

Trin said, "Did she send that list of references?"

I pretended not to hear her.

Mello added, "I'd like to see a list of the bands she's work-ing with. Who does Shining Stars represent?"

"Only most of the top bands in country, pop, and rock," I answered.

"Name one of them," Mello insisted.

"I don't know specific names," I admitted, looking at myself in the mirror. Way cute outfit. Way sad face. *It's not supposed to go like this*, I thought. *They're supposed to be excited.*

I felt like telling them about my chance to join Makayla's band. Makayla wouldn't be asking these kinds of questions. She'd have the contract signed and be on tour by now.

I heard Trin's door bang open. "Everybody get out here," she called from the store. "I want to see your outfits."

I opened the door and stepped out. They oohed and ahhed over my clothes.

I looked at Mello's blue lace shirt and Trin's pink jacket. "You look good too. Both of you," I said. Then I looked at the three of us reflected in the mirror. "Too bad it doesn't matter."

"What do you mean?" Mello asked.

I tugged off the denim jacket and tossed it to the floor in disgust. "Who cares how cute our clothes are when we're speeding down a dead-end road to nowhere?"

My phone signaled that I had a text message, and I ran back into the dressing room to check it. I had to dig through a pile of clothes, but I finally found it. The message was from Cole! It said:

pleez meet tomorrow at shelter 2 install stage and practice. 10 a.m.

I squealed and ran out to tell Trin and Mello. "That was Cole. The guys want to meet at the shelter tomorrow morning!"

"Ohwow! That's amazing! One call and you're like a different person. Totally happy."

I grinned. "Well, if we have to be stuck going nowhere, at least we can ride with KCH!"

chapter • 7

•••

wednesday

KCH showed up with a disassembled stage. It took several trips to get the parts from the borrowed truck to the
cafeteria.

I stood looking at the large sections and said, "This is, like,
the real deal."

Cole laughed. "Yeah. What did you think we were gonna do?"

I grinned. "I guess I thought we'd push some tables
together or something."

"We want to do this right," he explained. "This may be the
most important concert we'll ever do, you know?"

I frowned, thinking of all the places in the world the
Chosen Girls would probably never go. "Sí. Us too," I admitted. "Sad, isn't it?"

He looked confused. "What do you mean?"

"I mean, this is *Hopetown*."

"Oh, I know. It's hard to believe people right here in our own town are going hungry. It is sad. But that's why this is such an important concert."

That wasn't what I meant, but he left to haul the last piece over to Hunter, whose battery-powered screwdriver already filled the shelter with noise.

"We have a good idea how the stage goes together, but we're clueless on what to do for a backdrop. Any ideas?" Karson asked.

"I think it should be very subdued," Mello said. "This is a serious subject we're dealing with."

Trin shook her head. "I disagree. The setting should be vibrant and colorful. We're bringing hope—that's not sad or somber, it's exciting. It's something to celebrate."

"It doesn't seem right for people to walk into a homeless shelter and see balloons and confetti," Mello insisted.

"I never said balloons and confetti," Trin said. "But why give them gray and morbid? It's not a funeral home."

It felt like a good time to intervene. "What if we do both?" I asked.

They looked at me like I was crazy. "It could be symbolic. On one side, the backdrop is black. That fades to gray. Then colors start to come out of that—soft colors at first, but they get brighter and bolder so that the far side of the backdrop is a total explosion of color."

"Ohwow, I love it!" Trin squealed.

Mello hugged me. "You're brilliant, Harmony. This will be excellent."

When we had the design worked out, we started gathering materials. Mr. Camillo donated a ton of old bedsheets he had planned to throw out. He even had a few cans of leftover paint in different colors. We walked to a nearby hardware store to get the rest.

After we got back, we each grabbed two sheets and found a spot on the floor where we could spread them out. Mello showed us how to do a simple whipstitch, and we got busy sewing the sheets together.

"How can you sew and watch Cole at the same time like that?" Trin asked.

I explained, "I'm not watching Cole. I'm just trying to monitor the progress they're making on putting up the stage."

Mello cracked up. "Yeah, sure. You do that, Harmony."

"It is amazing, for reals," I insisted. "They almost have it put together."

Trin got to the end of her sheets and tied off the thread. "We're gonna practice today, right?"

"Yeah," Mello answered. "Maybe if we get this backdrop put together and painted, we can practice while it dries."

"What about lunch?" I asked. "I mean, this whole concert is about feeding the hungry, right? I'm hungry."

Across the room, Karson froze with the hammer in his hand. "Are you talking about lunch?" he asked.

"Wow!" Mello said. "You've got good ears."

He dropped his hammer and walked our way. "Just when it's about food. Let's take a break and get something to eat."

Lamont, Cole, and Hunter came right behind him.

"Where should we go?" I asked as I struggled to stand. "Ouch! My feet fell asleep!"

"Me too," Trin complained, stomping hers on the floor.

"What about Charlie's?" Cole asked. "We passed it on the way here, and it had a sign that said everything was homemade, including hand-breaded corn dogs and hand-patted burgers."

We agreed that it sounded great and followed Cole.

To get through the door of the restaurant, we had to pass two men sitting on the sidewalk, leaning against the brick wall. I tried not to stare at the first guy's matted brown hair, vacant eyes, and torn and stained clothes.

The second guy, who had greasy blond hair, spoke to us. "Can you spare a couple of bucks?"

My heart started racing. Real homeless people who needed our help! I reached for my purse.

Cole grabbed my arm. "Give us a minute, sir," he told the man. At the same time he gave me a little push toward the door.

I turned on him angrily. "Cole! The whole reason we're here is—"

"I know," he answered as we crowded inside. He lowered his voice. "But you can't just throw money at them. They'll probably go buy beer or drugs with it."

"So you don't want to help them?" I asked, amazed. "We're here working on a concert to feed the hungry, and we're going to walk right past two of them? Maybe they aren't alcoholics or addicts. Maybe they got laid off and can't find another job."

Trin started digging in her purse. "I'm with Harmony. We don't know their story. Besides, I don't think what they do with the money is our concern. They'll have to answer for that. But we'll have to answer for our response to them."

"Wait," Mello said. "I can see what Cole means. If we give them money, it is kind of our responsibility. And if they use it for drugs or cigarettes or whatever, how does that help them?"

Lamont spoke up. "What if we buy them some food? That way we aren't ignoring their need, but we aren't helping them kill themselves, either."

"Sounds good," Cole agreed. "I'll give up my fries and put in a couple of bucks."

"*Yo tambien,*" I agreed, handing two dollars to Lamont. When he had everyone's money, he ordered a couple of corn dogs, some fries, and two drinks. We all helped carry it out.

The men looked shocked. "You came back," the blond one said. "Thanks!"

The brown-haired guy just grabbed a corn dog and started in, attacking it like he hadn't eaten for a while.

We told them about the food pantry we were starting, and Cole wrote out two free passes to the concert. They said they'd check it out. Then we went back in to order for ourselves.

Before we ate, Lamont prayed for our food. "God, thanks for the blessing of a good meal. I don't think any of us will take that for granted again, after today. And thanks for giving us the ability to bless two of your children. Keep using us as we hold this concert and start the pantry. Amen."

Halfway through our meal Cole whispered, "Check out that woman over there with the corn dog. Have you ever seen anyone apply mustard so carefully?"

I looked at her and held back a giggle. She made a perfect line of mustard from top to bottom, then started back up with another straight line. She already had a couple of rows.

"Maybe she forgot she's going to have to eat it," I said. "All that careful work for—"

I stopped talking, because right then the woman stuck the corn dog to the side of her face.

"What was that?" Cole whispered, his aqua eyes huge with shock.

I covered my mouth to hold my laughter back. "She just slapped that thing against her ear!" I said, elbowing Mello. "Look! She got mustard all over herself."

We watched her grimace and pull the corn dog off her face. She laid it on the table and started pulling napkins out of the dispenser with one hand. With her other hand she dug through a large purse.

She finally pulled out a ringing cell phone and answered it.

Trin almost died laughing. "That's what happened! Her phone rang, and she answered her corn dog!"

The woman glanced in our direction, and we all looked away quickly, trying to act like we hadn't seen a thing. But every few minutes for the rest of lunch, one of us would start laughing and then we'd all bust up.

After lunch we went back to the shelter and finished stitching the sheets together. Next we started the fun part — painting. I handed Mello cans of black and gray. "You start on the depressing end. Trin and I will work on the happy side."

My knees ached by the time we got the whole thing done. I looked up and saw the guys heading over to check it out. "I hope they like it," I whispered to Trin.

"Hey! Great job!" Cole said. "This looks awesome."

"I like the colors taking over the gray," Lamont said. "Who thought of that?"

"Harmony did," Mello answered.

I shook my head. "We all did. It's symbolic of hope."

"Speaking of hope, I *hope* you're ready to practice," Karson said. "We've got to figure out how we're going to do this joint concert thing."

We stood and stretched. Trin said, "Sounds good. Let's make some music."

We hauled our equipment over to the stage. "It looks OK," Mello said, setting her drums on the floor beside it. "But I don't think I want to be the first one to walk on it."

"Oh, don't hurt me like that!" Karson yelled, pretending to stumble back. "This stage is solid. Put together by master craftsmen. Watch." He jumped onto the stage and did a back handspring across it.

"OK, then," Mello said. "I feel better." She handed a drum up to Karson and went back for another one.

"So, we've never done a whole concert with another band. Are we just gonna run it like two separate shows?" Trin asked, stepping onto a stool and then up onto the stage.

Hunter started plugging in wires. "What if one band opens," he suggested, "and then we do a few songs together, and the other band closes?"

Cole looked up from adjusting a monitor. "I think the last song needs to be all of us for maximum impact."

"OK, so we do what Hunter said, but then all get onstage for the final song," I said. "Sound good? And maybe we could play up the whole two-band thing somehow. Like we act surprised when the other band shows up."

"Yeah. That works," Trin agreed. "Why don't we open, since KCH opened at that beach concert."

"Whoa!" Cole said. "The Chosen Girls opening for KCH? We must really be in the big time."

"OK, we're not opening," I corrected. "We're going first."

Cole nodded. "We'll take it."

I pulled my guitar out of the case, and underneath it I found the list I had finally printed out. "Oh! I can't believe I forgot this. Trin, Mello, look," I said, carrying it over to them.

Trin took it. "What is it?"

"Just what it says. A list of the top ten ways the Chosen Girls can change the world! I've worked on it all week," I explained.

Mello walked up and read over Trin's shoulder: "Number one: provide farm equipment and training to AIDS orphans in Africa."

"I found this amazing organization that's doing that," I said. "I'm way glad, because I feel totally overwhelmed every time I read about what's going on over there. So many people are dying from AIDS. Millions of kids are left with no adults to take care of them. No one! So these people teach older kids how to farm, and then they can grow food for their younger brothers and sisters."

"Are you serious?" Trin asked. "I can't imagine being responsible for my little brother like that."

"I can't even imagine having to grow food for *myself*," Mello added. "Wow. That is way sad."

"But, if things were that bad and you were on your own, wouldn't you want someone to help?" I asked.

They nodded. "Definitely," Mello agreed.

Trin flipped through the pages. "Harmony, wait. There are, like, eight or nine pages here. I thought you said the top *ten* ways."

"Well, that's what I called it, but I couldn't narrow it down that far," I admitted. "Every time I go online I find something new, so I think there might be a few more than ten."

Mello grabbed the papers and turned to the last page. "Project number *forty-three*," she read aloud. "Harmony! Forty-three ways to change the world? Who do you think we are?"

"A really successful band," I answered. "A band that could be even more successful. And do bigger stuff than, than ..." I threw my hands up. "Than temporary stages in old high-school cafeterias. Way bigger than just one food pantry." I grabbed the papers.

"Look!" I said, pointing. "Number forty-three is packing care kits for victims of natural disasters. You think we should drop that one? Fine. *You* tell the victims of the next hurricane you don't care if they have clean drinking water and basic toiletry items."

"Hello?" Lamont said, storming onto the stage. "We can work out the details on saving the world later. Right now we have a concert to practice for, or there won't be even one food pantry." He waved his arm behind him to where Karson, Cole, and Hunter were sitting. "These fine gentlemen are waiting patiently, so perhaps you could show some respect by tuning up and getting this practice under way."

I rolled my eyes. Then I stomped back to my case. I threw the list inside and slammed it shut, feeling like I was slamming the lid on my dreams.

We played well for the first few songs. As we wrapped up the fourth one, Cole yelled, "Somebody's corn dog is ringing."

I couldn't help laughing as I hopped off the stage, digging in my purse until I came up with my phone. I looked at the screen — Larinda. I walked toward the back of the cafeteria, yelling, "Be right back," over my shoulder. When I was out of earshot, I answered. "Harmony speaking."

"Harmony. Larinda here. I hope your band is ready for worldwide recognition, because the time has come. I have the Chosen Girls contract all drawn up! When do you want to meet and sign this baby so we can get your first tour rolling?"

I looked at my band members waiting onstage. "Um, actually, we're in the middle of a practice right now. How about I talk to Trin and Mello and call you back later?"

"Just remember, this boat won't stay in port for long," she threatened. "If you want this, Harmony — and I know you do — you're going to have to take a leap of faith." Then she hung up.

"I hate the way she never says good-bye," I mumbled as I jogged back to the stage.

"Who was that?" Mello asked.

I grabbed my guitar and said, "We'll talk about it later. Right now these *fine gentlemen* are waiting and we have a concert to practice for."

chapter • 8

• • •

The next morning, I woke to the sound of an electric guitar playing "Amazing Grace." I rolled over and grabbed my phone. *"Hola,* Trin," I said.

"Yeah, Harmony. This is going to sound lame, but we rented this serious waterslide for my brother's birthday party. Actually, it's called a Slip and Dip. It's already here, and his party's not till tonight. I thought I'd see if—"

"Slip and Dip? Can I come play on it?"

"Well, yeah. That's why I called."

"Cool frijoles. Want me to call Mello?"

"Would you?"

"Sí!"

"Thanks."

"De nada."

I hung up and clicked on Mello's cross-eyed, fish face picture. I think I woke her up. She sounded way groggy. "Mmmm—hello?"

"Mello, Trin's got a huge Slip and Dip in her yard!"

"Has she called the police?"

"No, Mello. It's a good thing. Like a Slip'N Slide, but bigger and more fun."

"Oh. I'm happy for her, then," she said. And the line went dead.

I sighed and started digging around, looking for my swim-suit. At the same time, I clicked Mello's picture again. This time she sounded a little more awake.

"Hey, Harmony."

"You hung up on me!"

"Sorry. I thought we finished. Listen, I just want to sleep a little —"

I found my swimsuit and threw it on the bed. "But you can't, Mello. That's why I'm calling about the Slip and Dip," I explained.

She groaned. "See, I don't get that, Harmony. Why should something in *Trin's* yard mean *I* have to get out of bed?"

"Because she's invited us to play on it!" I answered, pull-ing my suit on. "Besides, it's almost ten. You've had enough sleep. All you have to do is put on your suit and get to Trin's! Can you meet us there in, like, fifteen minutes?" I got on my hands and knees to search the floor of my closet for flip-flops.

Mello asked, "Why would I want to leave my soft, warm bed to go run on something that has *slip* in the name? It's not like I need help slipping, Harmony."

"Then you'll be a pro," I said, tossing boots and sandals aside. "And you want to come because you love me, and you love Trin, and you cherish every moment you're able to spend with us."

"Harmony—"

"And we love you, and it wouldn't be the same without you," I finished, grabbing the purple flip-flops I had finally uncovered.

"You are so annoying," Mello complained. "But in a sweet way."

I walked down the hall to look for sunscreen in the bathroom. "So you're coming?"

I heard her sigh. "Yeah. I'm coming."

• • •

The Slip and Dip filled Trin's whole yard and part of the neighbor's.

"We had to promise them they could use it this afternoon," Trin explained. "Doesn't it look fun?"

"Way fun," I answered, checking out the huge inflated runway with red and blue inflated walls and rainbow-shaped arches overhead.

Trin clapped her hands happily. "When Mello gets here, we'll turn on the water. It sprays down from each little arch." She walked me to the end and pointed to a square pool about two feet deep. "And after you slide all the way, you fall in there."

Mello walked up and said, "I can't believe you got me up for this. How old are we?"

"Whatever," I answered. "This is awesome. But we need some music."

Trin ran over to the house. "Got it," she answered, turning on a huge boom box. Music poured out, and I couldn't help dancing.

"Now the water," Trin yelled over the tunes. She turned the faucet and the arches sprayed a mist onto the runway.

"Who's going first?" I asked.

"You can," Trin answered. "Get a running start."

I backed up across her neighbor's yard and yelled, "Ready?"

Trin called, "Go for it!"

I ran as hard as I could and dove onto the waterslide. I screamed as I hit the cold, wet plastic and felt the freezing spray on my back. I slid all the way to the end and — splash! I dove headfirst into the ice-cold water of the pool.

Trin and Mello ran over. "How was it?" Mello asked.

"Way cool," I answered. "You'll love it."

Trin went next. Then we begged until Mello finally said yes. She came up out of the pool saying, "I want to go again!"

"See?" I asked, running and diving. "Happens every time." I came up out of the pool and pushed wet hair out of my face.

"What happens every time?" Mello asked as Trin took her turn.

"You don't trust me at first. Then you finally give in, and you have to admit I'm right."

Mello yelled as she ran. "Whatever, Harmony." She slid to the end and came out laughing.

It was my turn, but I waited until Trin and Mello stood beside me. "I need you guys to trust me now," I said. "You'll find out I'm right. I know it."

Trin gathered a handful of her long hair and squeezed water out of it. "What? What's going on?"

I took a deep breath. "Larinda called. She has our contract all drawn up. All we have to do is meet her and sign it. We're on our way!"

Trin exploded. "No, Harmony. What are you thinking? How could you let things go this far?"

Mello leaned forward, her face inches from mine. "Why did she make a contract? We never asked for a contract. Did you do something, say something, that made her think we did?"

I felt my face flush as I thought about my meeting with Larinda. "No," I said. "When I took her the promo stuff, I told her you weren't sure yet."

"You took her stuff?" Trin asked. "Without talking to us about it? Why didn't you ask us first, Harmony?"

"I guess I knew what you'd say," I admitted. "So you're seriously not going to sign?"

Trin put her hands on her hips. "You amaze me. How can you sit there and act shocked? Have Mello or I ever given you the tiniest sliver of hope about this agent?"

"We've said no from the beginning, Harmony," Mello added.

I looked down. "I hoped you were afraid to believe it. I was. I didn't think a huge agency like Shining Stars would really take us. But now that they said yes—now that there's a real contract—I figured you would be as excited as I am."

Trin shook her head. "You figured wrong." She pointed at the huge inflatable in her yard. "Signing a contract isn't like trying out the Slip and Dip, Harmony. You're talking about all of us running headlong into a whole new life. Travel and tours. No more Hopetown, no more time for family ..."

"And you've never given us a reason to trust Larinda," Mello added. "Who knows what kind of plans she has for Chosen Girls? Slipping and falling is fun on this waterslide, but it's not fun to fall flat on your face in real life."

I blinked back tears. "But the list—all those people we could help if we made the big time—"

"I'm sick of your stupid list," Mello said. "It's like you're walking around with it so close to your face you can't even see the needs right around you."

The words stung like a slap to my face. "What do you mean?"

Mello rolled her eyes. "Hello? The food pantry?"

"*I thought of* the food pantry," I reminded her. "Why does everyone keep forgetting it was my idea?"

"Because what have you done about it since? Nothing. Even when you're at the shelter, in your mind you're somewhere else. Why?"

Trin joined in. "Yeah. What's the deal, Harmony? You talked us into the pantry, and we're psyched about it. But now it's like you've got bigger dreams and Hopetown doesn't even matter. Why do you think you have to feed every hungry child in the world?"

I gave up and let the tears roll down my cheeks. "Because I used to be one."

Mello said, "Huh?"

"I know how it feels, OK?" I said, angrily wiping the tears off my face. "I've been hungry. Not just hungry like when you're ready for the next meal. Hungry because you've missed a few meals and you don't know when the next one's coming."

Mello reached for my hand, but I pulled it away.

"When?" she asked. "In Peru?"

I shook my head. "In Peru we had tons of money. At least compared to everyone else. But my parents thought us kids would get a better education here, so they sold everything and came to the States. They didn't know how much everything would cost, though. The first two months of rent took all their savings, and that was for a broken-down little shack."

Trin sat on the grass and pulled me down beside her. She asked, "So what happened after that?"

"Papi looked for work. He thought he could get a good job because in Peru he owned his own business. He was a respected leader, you know? But here, everyone treated him like a *loco* — like some kind of idiot, since he didn't know English. He couldn't get hired anywhere. The money was gone, and they didn't know anyone. It was *muy malo* — very bad for a while."

Mello dropped to the ground beside me and whispered, "You never told me this."

"I guess I've tried to forget. It was before Papi became an air marshal. Before we moved to Hopetown. But the other day at the grocery store I saw these little kids and it all came back to me. I remembered begging Mamma for rice, for beans, or for bananas. I remembered the tears in her eyes when she had to say no."

Mello said, "Harmony, I feel awful. I can't believe I made fun of your list."

"I'm sorry too," Trin said. "Sorry you had to go through that, and sorry I didn't understand. I thought the whole agent thing was about you needing attention or something."

"So now that you know, do you get it? Can you see how hard it is for me to let this opportunity go? Our band really could change the world — or at least a lot of it," I said.

Trin twirled a strand of pink hair around her pointer finger. "What if we say maybe."

I jumped up, ready to scream.

"But only if you promise to concentrate on the Battle of the Bands first," Trin added. "It's tomorrow, and the winner gets five thousand dollars. That would go a long way toward some of the needs on your list."

I crossed my arms and thought about it. Larinda wouldn't be impressed about the delay, but it was the closest Trin had come to agreeing. Besides, winning the contest was one of the assignments Larinda gave me. "What do you think, Mello?" I asked.

"About saying maybe?" she asked.

"Sí," I agreed. "Just opening your mind to the possibility."

She tapped a beat on her crossed legs. "OK. I'm good with that. But we do need to talk about the contest," Mello insisted. "We've been so busy with the shelter, we've hardly practiced."

"It will probably be the biggest crowd we'll ever play for," Trin pointed out.

Mello groaned. "Don't remind me!"

"I'm thinking about it in terms of changing the world," Trin explained with a wink in my direction. "Can we pray that God will speak through our music? If the people listening hear our message, I'll be satisfied. Even if we don't win."

I held my hands out to them. "How can I argue with that?"

chapter • 9

• • •

On the way to the contest the next day, Trin asked, "What's wrong, Harmony? You look kind of green. Are you nervous?"

I nodded.

Mello said, "Now you're freaking me out. *I'm* the one who gets nervous, not you. Chill out—it's only twenty thousand people."

She smiled when I shrugged, unsure how to explain it wasn't the crowd or the contest that bothered me.

I was scared of running into Larinda.

I hadn't called her back, and I had no idea how to explain why. I could blame it on Trin and Mello, but would that help? They belonged to the Chosen Girls too. She'd think they were immature and unprepared for success, and then what?

Once we pulled up to "security" behind the stages, I forgot to worry. We had to show our IDs to get backstage passes. They also gave us loads of papers—schedules, rules, even tourist information for L.A. Next we unloaded, making about a hundred trips between the Suburban and the tiny piece of lawn marked Chosen Girls.

The place looked like a circus — yellow plastic ribbons tied to metal stakes divided the wide green lawns into sections. Every piece of grass seemed to have someone on it warming up on drums, tuning a guitar, or practicing the keyboard. It sounded wonderfully out of control.

Looking around, I felt better and worse at the same time. The odds of running into Larinda had to be almost zero. On the other hand, most of the people in the roped-off area had come to compete. That meant Shining Stars had plenty of bands to choose from if I couldn't get Trin and Mello onboard soon.

"Harmony?" Trin asked, snapping her fingers in front of my face. "Did you hear me?"

I blinked and focused on her face. "No, sorry, I was . . . thinking."

She grabbed my shoulders and shook them. "You promised, Harmony. Just for today, try to actually *be here with us*."

"And what a good place to be," Mello whispered. She jerked her head to the right. "Look!"

I looked and had to cover my mouth to stop the scream. "It's Drake's Passage!" I squealed.

"Ohwow!" Trin exclaimed. "The coolest boy band of all time, maybe twenty-five feet from us!"

"But what are they doing here?" Mello asked. "They can't compete, can they?"

"They're an exhibit band," Lamont explained. "They're performing tonight, while the judges tally scores."

"That's right," I said. "I read it on the contest info, but I never dreamed they'd be, like, right there!"

"Ohwow, ohwow, ohwow!" Trin said. "They're coming this way!"

Mello panicked. "What do we do? Do we say something? Ask for autographs?"

"No," I said. "That's what all the immature, irritating fans do. Act cool. Pretend you don't even care."

"But, Harmony!" Trin said.

"Silencio, amigas," I hissed. "And stop staring!"

"We can't even look?" Mello whined.

Lamont laughed. "I'm telling KCH."

I tried to appear busy with my guitar. But after a few moments, I couldn't stand it. I glanced up just as Julian, the lead singer with incredible jet-black curls and amazing green eyes, walked by. He looked right at me! What could I do?

"Hey," I said. "Love your music."

Julian nodded and said thanks. Then he read the paper that marked our spot. "Hey! You're the Chosen Girls!"

I nodded. "Yeah, uh, we are."

"Lawson, Carlos," he called. The drummer and bass player loped over. "You won't believe this," Julian said. "This is that band we heard on the radio yesterday."

"No way," Carlos said, running a hand through his thick blond hair. "You rock."

Lawson smiled his toothpaste commercial smile at Trin. "I hope you're doing that song today — 'You've Chosen Me.'"

"Absolutely," Trin answered, her wide smile matching his.

"Cool!" Lawson said.

"Hope today goes well for you," Julian added. "What time are you on?"

Mello fumbled for the schedule, since none of us seemed capable of remembering our assigned time. "Uh ... uh ... it's here somewhere. Um, here it is. Six fifteen," she finally announced.

"We'll be cheering for you," Carlos said. He gave a sweet two-fingered salute, and they walked away.

"I love being backstage!" I whispered.

Mello looked dazed. "They knew us! They heard us on the radio!"

"And they liked us!" Trin added. "How cool is that?"

Lamont said, "I hate to interrupt your squeal session, but you may want to warm up if you're gonna uh, um, um, do 'You've Chosen Me' at uh, uh, uh, six fifteen."

I pounded his arm.

"He's right," Trin admitted. "We have to rock. Drake's Passage is going to be watching us!"

"They aren't the only ones who'll be watching," Mello mumbled. "Snob Mob at two o'clock."

"Two o'clock?" I asked, looking at my watch. "It's five fifteen."

Mello rolled her eyes at me. "Not time, Harmony. Position. Imagine you're in the middle of a big clock on the ground with noon straight ahead, and just look where the two would be."

I did.

"Oh. Got it," I said as I spotted Makayla's silvery blonde mane. Even from across the field, I could tell from her body language that she was barking out orders to her band members. "I wonder where the KCH guys are. I hope they come in ahead of Makayla this time."

We ran through the whole set and then headed to the Port-a-Potties for our last bathroom break. There were only three, and several people in line for each one, so I decided to go somewhere else. Unfortunately, that decision brought me into direct contact with Makayla.

"Signed any contracts lately?" she asked, stepping in front of me and blocking my path. "I'm assuming you finally talked Trin and Mello into it since you haven't called," she snapped.

"Actually, no, we haven't signed yet," I admitted.

Her steel-gray eyes narrowed, and she lifted her chin. "I am *not* used to being stood up, Harmony. Are you joining the Makayla Simmons band or sticking with your loser buddies?"

"My loser buddies and I won the last contest, Makayla," I reminded her.

She flipped her hair. "And what have you done since?"

Lamont interrupted. "Sorry to disturb you. I can tell you're having fun and all, but you're on in less than twenty minutes, Harmony." He kept walking, and I shrugged at Makayla and followed him.

"Thanks, Lamont," I whispered to his back. "I needed to be rescued."

"Thought so," he answered, slowing down so I could walk beside him. "You don't need to listen to her trash talk right before you perform."

I made it back to our spot and picked up my guitar to tune one more time before going onstage.

Thunk!

"Ack!" I yelled. "My E string just broke!"

"No way, Harmony!" Trin yelled. "We have, like, five minutes. And where is Mello?"

I dug around for another string. "I thought she was with you!"

Trin unplugged her guitar and grabbed a drum. "She was in line beside me, but I haven't seen her since. I figured she'd come back." She looked around frantically. "We've got to start carrying stuff to the stage. It's, like, a mile from here!"

"Let me help," Lamont said. "Harmony, fix your string and then find Mello. Trin, start hauling."

Trin and Lamont took off. I restrung and tuned, then headed for the line of portable bathrooms. I yelled at the top of my lungs, "Mello? Are you in there somewhere?"

I heard a weak answer from the middle building, so I ran to it. "Mello?"

"I'm in here," she squeaked.

I leaned against the door and said, "Mello, we're onstage in"—I looked at my watch—"two minutes!"

"I know," she answered. "I'm so sorry. I can't come out. I just don't feel well at all."

"Because you're nervous?" I asked.

"Well, duh. This place is huge, Mello. And Drake's Passage is here! I think I'm going to barf."

"Okay, so barf," I said, "but Drake's Passage will hear that Chosen Girls can't perform because Melody McMann is stuck in a Port-a-Potty."

"Good point," she answered. The door flew open, whacking me on the nose. Mello said, "Oh! Sorry, Harmony. Are you OK?"

I grabbed my nose with one hand and her arm with the other. "We don't have time to worry about it," I told her, sprinting toward the stage. "We're already on the clock."

"What about my drums?"

"Trin and Lamont carried everything for us," I explained.

We bounded up the steps. Trin and Lamont had gotten everything in place, and they were plugging in the last of the cords.

"Ohwow," Trin said, "am I glad to see you two. The judges are watching us set up and tear down, so look calm and orderly, like everything's going according to plan."

"Basically," Lamont added, "smile like you aren't freaking."

"Got it," I said. Mello just nodded and pressed her lips together in a fake smile.

Lamont glanced at his watch. "The timer's only been running for seven minutes, so we're OK. Mello, start warming up. Trin, Harmony, finish tuning. Break a leg!" He disappeared down the steps, and Mello and I headed toward our spots.

"Wait, Chosen Girls, come here," Trin said. "Let's pray."

"Here?" Mello asked. "Onstage, in front of everyone?"

Trin answered, "I think we need to." She held her hands out to us.

"God, you know we're feeling some serious pressure right now," Trin prayed. "Help us. We want to bring you glory." She squeezed my hand.

I thought of Larinda and added, "Help us do well, God. We need to win." I squeezed Mello's hand.

She prayed, "Um, God, I think all of us need help to remember this isn't really about the Chosen Girls. It isn't even about the Battle of the Bands. It's about you and a chance to hook people up with your love. Amen."

We put our hands in the middle and pumped them up and down three times before we yelled, "Chosen Girls rock!" Then we ran to our places and started the first song.

By the time we got halfway through the first verse, I couldn't stop smiling. We sounded incredible! I looked at

Mello and she winked at me. I winked back, so relieved to have her onstage.

The crowd got way into it. They put their hands in the air and clapped and danced and sang along, and that energized us.

Trin added some extra vocals that totally rocked, and a new guitar riff. I responded with a crazy new pattern on my bass. Usually onstage in front of a few thousand people is not the place to try something new, but it just fit. It felt like we could do no wrong.

The whole set went that way. We changed to our super suits and closed with our signature song, "You've Chosen Me." The crowd went crazy-wild.

We wrapped it up and managed to clear the stage in time. As we pulled the last piece of equipment offstage, the timer showed thirty-five seconds left.

We jumped and hugged and screamed and relived every second.

"We have to win!" Trin said. "We've never rocked like that."

"It was excellent!" Mello agreed. "I'm so glad you dragged me onstage, Harmony."

I hugged her again. "See? You were made for this, Mello. We all were. We should be playing for crowds like this every weekend. Maybe three times a weekend. I'm calling Larinda right now!" I started digging through my stuff, hunting for my phone.

Trin grabbed my arm. "Harmony, don't ruin this perfect moment by bringing that agent into it."

"You promised, Harmony," Mello said. "No agent today, remember?"

"I promised to focus on our competition," I corrected. "We're finished now, so we can move on."

"Wait," Trin said. "Why don't you at least let them announce the winners first? Winning a Battle of the Bands this huge would have to make us worth more."

"True," Mello agreed. "If you want the big bucks, it makes sense to wait."

I rolled my eyes. "Wait, wait, wait. Why does this sound familiar? I'm tired of waiting," I complained. "You set me up, didn't you? You never meant to sign. You never will. We're going to be seventy-five with arthritis and gray hair, and you'll still be telling me to wait!"

I pulled away from them and started running. I weaved between people and around people, not caring where I ended up as long as it was far away from Trin and Mello.

I ran right into a boy in a college sweatshirt. He immediately yelled, "Look! A superhero!" I had forgotten I had on my super suit.

Someone else said, "Oh, help me, hero! Save me!"

"I can't," I mumbled, still running. "I can't help anyone. I have to wait."

When I reached the fence that separated backstage from the parking lot, I stopped. "A dead end," I whispered. "That fits." I banged on the chain link that kept me from going any farther. I kicked it until my foot hurt, and then I leaned against the mesh and cried.

When I heard someone call my name, I looked up.

And into the glacier-green eyes of Larinda Higgins.

chapter • 10

•••

"Harmony, I expected to hear from you. You said you would call back and schedule a time to sign the contract," Larinda began. "I realize you are young, but I expect a certain amount of professionalism from those who hope to work with Shining Stars. I can only assume there has been some sort of family tragedy or perhaps a serious illness that has delayed your response?"

I couldn't tell if she wanted me to answer her or not, so I just crossed my arms and stood there.

"When do you plan to sign?" she asked.

I wiped the tears off my face. "Well, you're right. Kind of right. There is a, um, problem," I admitted.

"Yes?" she prompted.

I pulled my eyes away from hers and looked at the fence again. "Trin and Mello want to wait a bit longer," I finally admitted.

"Wait?" she asked. "Wait for what? Look around, Harmony. Do you think you're the only band with talent?"

I shook my head.

"*Why* do they want to wait?" she asked.

I shrugged. "Trin is afraid you'll try to change our band."

"I thought you were the band manager," Larinda said. "Does Trin have control issues?"

"No!" I answered, turning back to her. "She's really good at organizing stuff. It's her gift. She doesn't—"

"And the other one?" Larinda interrupted. "What's Melody's problem with signing?"

I took a deep breath and answered, "Mello is kind of quiet. She doesn't love all this limelight stuff like—"

"Stage fright?" Larinda asked. "It's not possible. How could she have gotten this far?"

"She handles it," I answered. "Actually she's the bravest person I know, because she goes onstage and rocks no matter how scared she is."

We both listened as the announcer at the contest declared, "Awards will be presented in fifteen minutes."

Suddenly, I didn't care what Larinda thought of us. I just wanted to be with Trin and Mello. Besides, what would it look like when the announcer called Chosen Girls for first place, and the bass player was missing?

"We'll talk later," I told Larinda and went to find my band. I got to our backstage spot as the announcer said, "Welcome to the biggest ever L.A.-area Battle of the Bands for Teens!"

I couldn't see them anywhere. I panicked and ran around screaming, "Trin! Mello!" before I realized we had a reserved place in the audience for the award ceremony. I could hear sponsors being thanked as I found our spot in the bleachers and hugged my friends. They looked surprised, but they hugged me back. I slid into my seat just as the announcer said, "Third place: the Chosen Girls!"

I found myself blinking under a spotlight.

Around us, people screamed and cheered.

Third place?

The Chosen Girls never got third place. In every contest so far, we'd been declared the grand winner.

The news finally sank in, and I whispered, "Act happy!" to Trin and Mello. I forced myself to smile and wave.

Trin blinked at me and said, "Oh! Right!" She grabbed Mello's shoulders and jumped up and down.

"That's enough," Lamont told us. "Go get your prize."

We ran to the stage and smiled fake smiles when they handed us a big, shiny trophy and a check for five hundred dollars. The presenter motioned for us to stay onstage while they gave out the rest of the awards, so we had to keep acting happy. That got harder when they announced first place: "The Makayla Simmons band!"

It felt like a punch in the stomach. "Makayla?" I whispered to Trin. "First place?"

"Keep smiling," she hissed through her teeth.

Makayla and her followers pranced onto the stage to accept their check.

"That's just what she needs," Mello whispered. "More money."

The awards finally wrapped up. Trin said exactly what I was thinking: "Let's get out of here." We started for the steps.

Makayla stepped in front of us.

"Chosen Girls," she said, looking down her pug nose at us. "Congratulations on *third* place."

Trin said, "Thanks, Makayla. Congratulations to you too." Then Trin tried to push past her.

Makayla said, "Don't leave yet. I need to talk to your bass player. Harmony, have you decided what you're going to do?"

I shook my head. I put a finger to my mouth to shush her, and with my eyes I begged her not to say anything.

"Trin?" Makalya said. "Did you and Mello know Harmony and I have been talking for a while now? See, my bass player is moving next week, creating an opening in the Makayla Simmons band."

"I'll call you later, Makayla," I said. I pushed Trin and Mello forward and said, "Let's go."

"No, this is interesting," Mello said. "I'd like to hear what Makayla has to say."

Makayla lifted her huge trophy a little higher. "Well, Harmony shared with me how she wants to be part of a band with a future. She isn't convinced that the Chosen Girls have what it takes. She said the two of you are really holding her back, you know? So she asked about joining my band."

"Makayla, you're the one who—," I began.

Trin reeled around to face me. "You talked to Makayla about joining *her* band?"

"Well, yes, but—"

Mello blinked back tears. "You told her *we* were holding you *back*?"

I groaned in frustration. "Not exactly, but—"

Trin and Mello looked at each other and then at me.

"Oh, this is classic!" Trin said, her hands on her hips. "Couldn't figure out how to tell us, huh? Well, don't bother. You don't have to quit the Chosen Girls. We'll save you that heartache."

"Yeah," Mello agreed, wiping the back of her hand across her eyes. "I can't believe you, Harmony. If that's what you think of us—you're out."

They walked off together, leaving me with Makayla. "Well, that worked out nicely," she said. "Now you don't have any agonizing decision to make. Not that it would have been hard to choose my band, after we got first place today!"

She caressed her trophy. "So. Back to business. Our first practice will be Monday at 9:00 a.m. in my dad's studio. Don't even think about being late. Come ready to work hard and pay attention. You're going to get schooled in how Makayla Simmons runs her *first-place* band."

I couldn't wait to get home. I needed to escape—to find some kind of refuge from Makayla, and the agent, and my angry friends. But first I had to survive the silent ride in the Suburban.

Back home, I flung myself on my bed. How had things gotten so out of control?

All I wanted was to help little kids who didn't have enough to eat. Now we wouldn't be helping anyone, because I had destroyed the Chosen Girls and lost my two best friends in the process.

When I ran out of tears, I sat up and reached for my laptop. I pulled up the list of the Top Ten Ways the Chosen Girls Can Change the World. One by one I highlighted each item and deleted it.

When I got to number thirty-four (sending used eyeglasses to third-world countries), an email popped up:

> Harmony,
> How I wish the Chosen Girls had come in first today! Still, third
> place is excellent in a contest as large as the L.A. Battle of the

Bands. The areas of concern we discussed today — hesitancy to
yield control, fear of performing in public, and your own lack of
professionalism — are more of a problem.

Still, I feel compelled to give you a chance. I think the three
of you have enough raw talent that with some adjustments
you could become the band I envision — fresh, invigorating,
inspiring. And wildly successful.

And so I offer you one final opportunity. I will be available
Sunday afternoon. You can meet me then to sign the contract.
If you choose not to, there is another highly talented female
band that is anxious to sign.

Please see the attached list of possible concert venues and tour
schedules available if you decide to work with Shining Stars.

Signed,

Larinda Higgins

I opened the attachment. New York City. Washington, D.C.
Boston. Dallas. London. Paris.

London and Paris????

I closed the file and started a new email. I wrote:

Dear Larinda,

I am sorry to inform you that I am no longer the manager for
the Chosen Girls. In fact, the band broke up this evening.

Best of luck to you and the other band. I'm sure you'll all go far.

Sincerely,

Harmony

Then I slammed the lid of my laptop closed and walked
away. I didn't want my falling tears to fry the keyboard.

chapter • 11

...

As soon as I woke up, I knew what I needed to do.

I wasn't sure I could get anyone to answer the phone, so I sent out text messages:

super deluxe apology 2 b offered in the shed at 10:30 a.m. pleez come.

I got there early and let myself in. I paced around, watching the door.

No one came.

What if they stood me up? I deserved it, I knew. But surely they wouldn't do that to me.

I picked up a magazine and leafed through it. I glanced at titles like: "When Your Best Friend Is a Jerk," and "Who Can You Trust?" I decided to stop reading and just look at the pictures — but then the pictures got blurry as my eyes filled with tears.

I threw the magazine down and flipped open my phone. No messages. I checked the time: 10:37. So that was it.

They weren't going to come.

I closed my eyes and tried to imagine life without Mello. I couldn't. We've been best friends since second grade, and Mello is part of every happy memory I've made since then.

And Trin? She only showed up last summer, but her energy and enthusiasm changed everything about my life in Hopetown. I love the way she challenges me to do more than I think I can. The way she dreams big, then makes the dreams come true.

I reached for a tissue and blew my nose, loudly. Then I sighed and walked slowly to the door.

It flew open, and Trin burst in. Mello came right behind her. "I just got your message!" Trin yelled.

"Me too!" Mello added. "I was afraid you'd leave."

"I was about to," I admitted. "I didn't think you were coming."

Trin flopped onto the couch. "You should know me better than that. I never miss a chance to see someone grovel."

Mello sat beside her. "No doubt. So now we're here. Start groveling."

I stood in front of the couch and held up my pointer finger. "First of all, I want you to know I didn't go to Makayla. She came to me," I explained.

Trin turned to Mello. "Does that sound like an apology?" she asked.

"No," Mello answered. "It sounds more like self-defense."

"Is there room for self-defense in a superdeluxe apology?" Trin asked.

Mello shook her head. "I don't think so. Especially not right at the beginning. Try again, Harmony."

I rolled my eyes and tried not to grin. "How's this: I acted like a major jerk, and I'm *so* sorry!"

Mello turned to Trin and asked, "I don't know. What do you think?"

"Better," Trin said. "But something's not quite right about her posture. Shouldn't she be, like, down on her knees or something?"

"That would definitely help," Mello agreed.

"You two are awful!" I declared. They made evil eyes at me, and I quickly added, "But not as awful as me, of course." I knelt down, clasped my hands together and blinked up at them. "I am the lowliest of all sorry excuses for a friend. I betrayed your trust by conversing with the enemy. I now realize the hugeness of my mistake. I beg you to let me back into your lives! Let me back into Chosen Girls!"

"Now that was good," Trin declared.

Mello nodded. "I liked it too. Much better."

"Was it the kneeling that made the difference?" Trin asked.

Mello shrugged. "I'm not sure. It may have been the big, pitiful eyes."

"So?" I interrupted. "You forgive me?"

They both jumped up and grabbed me into a group hug.

"Of course!" Trin answered.

"Definitely," Mello agreed.

It felt so good to have their arms around me, I started crying happy tears. Then Mello started bawling, and finally Trin joined us—all three of us sobbing and laughing and wiping our eyes and our noses.

"I missed you!" I told them.

"We missed you too," they said.

"And I'm ready to appreciate what we've got," I continued. "The Chosen Girls are way awesome, just the way we are. I'm going to focus on the fund-raising concert for the food pantry. Seriously. I'm not going to worry about changing the world or touring in Europe. And I'm not going to mention that agent again, ever."

"Really?" Mello asked.

"Sí," I answered.

"Oh," Trin said, falling back onto the couch. "That's too bad."

"What?" I asked.

"Well, Mello and I talked about it last night . . . ," Trin began.

I looked at Mello.

She picked up one of her purses and messed with the strap. "We, uh, decided maybe you were right. That getting an agent is our next logical move as a band."

My legs felt weak. I sat on the edge of the coffee table.

"It makes sense," Trin continued. "God has given us this incredible opportunity. Who are we to say no? I mean, why not reach as many people as we can?" She winked. "Even if that means giving up some of my control."

Mello smiled. "And even if it means performing in front of thousands and feeling sick to my stomach every time," she added.

"So why aren't you whipping out your phone? Calling Larinda right now?" Trin asked.

Mello looked at me sideways and said, "I figured you'd at least jump around and scream. What's going on?"

I buried my face in my hands. "It's just that, well, I'm not totally sure the agent thing is still an option after last night," I told them.

Trin nodded. "The third-place disaster. Yeah, we thought of that. You think she doesn't want us anymore?"

"Oh, she did," I admitted. "Even after third place. She sent an email last night giving us one last chance. She said we could meet her Sunday afternoon and sign."

Mello sat up straighter. "Perfect!"

"Not perfect," I said with a sigh. "I emailed her back and told her the band had split up. I told her to go ahead and sign some other band she's been talking to — probably Makayla's."

"No!" Trin said, jumping up off the couch. "The Makayla Simmons band is going to get our contract?"

"And do our concerts and our tours ...," I complained.

"Wait," Mello said. "Don't give up yet. Harmony, you've got to call her. Beg, plead, whatever it takes. Get her to meet *us,* not Makayla, on Sunday."

I pulled out my phone and clicked on Larinda's number.

"Larinda Higgins of Shining Stars speaking," she answered.

"Hi, Larinda. It's me, Harmony."

"Yes?"

"I was just wondering, um, if you already signed a contract with anyone else," I asked. I moved to the other side of the shed so Mello and Trin couldn't hear her response.

"Harmony," she said. "Do I have to remind you we currently have no working relationship?"

I swallowed. "I'd like to change that. If it's still possible, I mean. Our band is back together, and everyone wants to meet Sunday to sign — if it isn't too late."

"I'm so sorry," she said. "It's ironic, really. If you had called just a bit earlier! I returned only moments ago from dropping off a contract to the lead singer and manager of the other band I've spoken to you about. You may know her. Makayla Simmons. Her band won first place at the Battle of the Bands yesterday."

"Yes, I know her. Well, thanks any—"

"I'll be in touch if for some reason that contract falls through."

I pushed End and shook my head.

Mello picked up her purse again. "Oh, well. We can always sell more purses," she said with a smile.

"And necklaces," Trin added, wandering over to the shelf where I'd been keeping my beads. "We only need to sell, what? A few hundred a month?"

•••

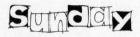

Sunday morning as I dressed for church my phone rang.

"Harmony. Larinda here. It turns out that Shining Stars will not be able to represent Makayla Simmons. Are the Chosen Girls prepared to sign a contract today?"

"Cool frijoles!" I yelled. "I mean, sí. I mean, yes, absolutely. Definitely."

"I can meet you at three o'clock. You name the place," she said.

"The Java Joint," I answered. "Three o'clock. We'll be there! Thank you, Larinda!"

I met Trin and Mello at the Java Joint at 2:55, grabbed some frozen drinks, and chose a booth. I reached in my pocket and pulled out a folded paper. "Look at this!" I said. "Larinda sent this list of possible concert and tour venues. I printed it out to show you today."

"New York City?" Trin squealed, reaching for my hand and squeezing it.

Mello put her hands over her mouth and barely whispered, "London! I've always wanted to go to London!"

"I know!" I said, bouncing in my seat. "And Paris! Could we have some serious fun-o-rama in Paris?"

"You know it. We're going to rock the *world*, for reals!"

Mello tapped a beat on the table. "I can't wait. What time is it?"

I checked my phone. "Five after," I answered. "I'm surprised she's late. She's really into being professional."

"So we need to act like we know what we're doing," Mello said.

"Right," I agreed. "Like we sign contracts every day. Oh! I bet that's her!" I pointed to a bright red sports car pulling into a parking space out front.

"OK, everybody," I said, "be cool."

Larinda pushed the door open and stood for a moment scanning the restaurant. She wore a red micro-miniskirt and a shiny white jacket over a silk cami.

"That's professional?" Trin whispered.

I shrugged. "Maybe for the music industry," I answered.

Larinda spotted us and teetered over to our table on three-inch spike heels that clicked against the tile with each step. She flashed us a huge smile. "Hello, Chosen Girls. Harmony, we've met. Trinity, Melody, I'm Larinda Higgins." She reached out and shook their hands. "I am in desperate need of coffee, so how about if you take a look at the contract while I place my order?"

She lifted her briefcase to the edge of the table, and then frowned at our drinks. We quickly picked them up.

She nodded, popped open her briefcase, and pulled out an inch-high pile of paper.

"Don't be intimidated," she said, placing the stack on the table. "It's mostly disclaimers and what we in the business call *legalese*—a bunch of legal mumbo jumbo. You'll see that as you glance through it. Nothing to be concerned about."

Then she wobbled over to the counter, her shoes clicking as she walked.

I picked up the first page and read aloud:

"We, the Chosen Girls (hereafter referred to as BAND) do hereby enter into this binding agreement with Ms. Larinda Higgins (hereafter referred to as AGENT) on this _____ day of _____ in the year _____."

"So far, so good," Trin said.

Mello nodded. "Yeah, that part makes sense."

"That's the last part that does," I warned them as I scanned the next paragraph. We were completely lost by the time Trin whispered, "Here she comes."

We looked up and smiled.

Larinda reached into her briefcase and brought out four pens. "All right, then, are you ready to sign?" she asked, sliding into the booth beside me.

"We only got to the second page," Trin said.

"Did you try to read it *word for word*?" When we nodded, she rolled her eyes. "Oh, please." She put the pens down, grabbed the stack of papers and said, "Let me walk you through it. There's very little in here you actually need to read, so I'll summarize."

She flipped through pages so fast it looked like snow flurries right there in the Java Joint. She said stuff like, "These pages talk about avoiding objectionable content in your songs. These pages talk about dressing appropriately. These pages say you're agreeing to my terms."

In just a few minutes, she made it to the last page. "And here's where you sign," she said, tapping a long red nail on the blank lines.

"Ohwow, I'm not sure I followed all that," Trin admitted. "Should we, like, take it home and look it over first?"

Larinda slid out of the booth and stood up. She adjusted the stack of papers to get them all straight. "I know signing is your decision, but I've already spent considerable time waiting for Harmony to call this meeting," she said, reaching for her briefcase. "I thought you were ready to sign. If you aren't, you shouldn't have met me here today." She opened the briefcase and put the contract inside.

"Wait!" I said. "We're ready." I reached for a pen.

"Me too," Trin agreed.

Larinda looked at Mello, who said, "Definitely."

"Fine, then." Larinda handed out the other pens. "I am your agent. My whole job is to represent you and look out for your best interests. If you can't trust me, who can you trust?"

After we had all signed and initialed everywhere Larinda told us to sign and initial on two different copies of the contract, we sat back and smiled at each other. "That's it, then," I said. "We're officially headed for stardom!"

Trin looked at her watch. "Ohwow. It's three forty-five. We've got to get to the shelter."

"Tonight's our fund-raising concert," I explained, handing Larinda a flyer. "Do you want to come?"

Larinda gathered papers and stacked them. "I may come by. I'd like to go over a few more details with you. What time do you expect to finish up?"

"Nine-ish," Trin answered, sliding out of the booth.

Larinda smiled. "Great. Expect me then."

As we walked out of the Java Joint, Trin said, "So, Harmony, do you still have that list of all the ways we're going to change the world?"

"Oh, no!" I exclaimed. "I deleted most of it after the Battle of the Bands."

Mello linked an arm through mine and grinned. "Then you better start working on a new one. We're going to need some worthy causes to spend our unlimited funds on!"

Trin smiled her brightest megawatt smile as she hooked elbows on my other side. "Maybe we can work on the list together. On the airplane." She winked at me. "I hear the flight to Paris is pretty long!"

...

chapter 12

Still Sunday

I found Trin and Mello backstage before the concert at the shelter.

"How awesome is this?" I asked. "Our last big local show. Then we're off! New York, London, Paris—here we come!"

"But you're choosing to be *here* first, right?" Mello prompted. "Not just physically present, but actually aware of what's going on around you."

I caught sight of Cole rushing past, doing last-minute setup. I grinned and said, "Sí. I am oh-so-happily aware of what's going on around me."

Trin shoved me. "That's not what we mean, and you know it."

Lamont peeked around our backdrop and said, "Have you seen the back wall?"

"What?"

He grabbed my arm and tugged me toward the front of the stage. He pulled our painted sheet back a few inches and pointed. "Through there."

"Cool frijoles!" I exclaimed. "The place is packed! And those two men from Charlie's restaurant are in the front row."

"Yeah. Cool that they showed up. Them and the rest of Hopetown. The captain's worried about fire codes. But you aren't looking at the back wall," he reminded me.

I looked past the people and caught my breath. "Are those pyramids what I think they are?"

He smiled. "Yeah. Cole came up with the idea of stacking the cans that way."

"They almost reach the ceiling!" I said, feeling my smile grow wider. "And there are—what? Ten pyramids? Twelve? How many cans of food do you think that is?"

"The guys stopped counting at one thousand," he said. "I'd call that a decent start for the food pantry."

Cole jogged up and said, "Everything ready?"

"All set," Lamont assured him.

"You're on in five," Cole told me. "The captain wants to introduce your band."

I asked, "Do you think we can really pull off the new closing song? We haven't had much time to practice together."

He nodded. "It's going to rock."

I said thanks and went back to pray with Trin and Mello. We prayed that God would take complete control of the evening—from the music to the product sales. After prayer, we heard Mr. Camillo's voice over the sound system.

"Thank you, Hopetown, for coming out tonight. You're here because you have neighbors who need your help to have even their basic needs met—things most of us take for granted, like food and shelter. It warms my heart to know you care, and I'm sure it touches their hearts as well.

"As we start off the evening, please join me in welcoming the Chosen Girls!"

We ran to our instruments as Lamont swirled different-colored spotlights all over the stage. The crowd responded immediately, and I didn't have to concentrate on having a good time. I couldn't help but have a blast. Our first two songs went great.

When people finally stopped clapping, Trin talked about the shelter and all the services it offered. Then we sang "Love Lessons," with Lamont's PowerPoint playing on the huge screen behind us.

It got even more fun after that, because KCH came running out. Hunter's drums were already onstage, so he went straight to them. Cole and Karson quickly plugged in their guitars. Then they all looked around and acted like they were surprised to see us.

Cole launched into the little sketch we had practiced. He said, "Hey, Karson, isn't this where we're supposed to perform tonight?"

"Yeah. The Cleft of the Rock Shelter," Karson answered.

Cole looked at Hunter. "What time is it?"

Hunter checked his watch. "Seven forty-five."

"That's the right time, and we're in the right place," Cole said. "But, uh ... there's another band onstage."

Trin spoke into her mike. "Is there some kind of problem?"

"It's just that, well, we planned to do a concert here tonight," Cole explained.

Trin nodded. "I see. So you want us to leave? Is that it?"

"No, um, I didn't mean —"

"Because we were here first, you know," she pointed out.

Cole looked at his friends and said, "Wow, this is awkward."

People in the audience chuckled.

"We could try a song together," Karson suggested.

"With two drummers, two bass players, and two lead electric guitars?" Trin asked.

Cole shrugged. "I'm willing to try it."

Trin looked at Mello and me. We nodded. "OK," she said. "Let's see what happens."

Hunter tapped four beats and we broke into "Revolution," a song KCH had taught us. Playing with that many musicians felt totally wild, but it sounded even more amazing in concert than at our practice sessions. And I *so* loved having Cole on the same stage.

We sang two more songs with them, and then Trin said, "Well, this has been fun. But I guess we should let these guys have the stage for a while."

We left the stage and just enjoyed their music for a few songs. Then Cole said, "You know, I don't think we can do this closing song alone. I wonder if we could get the Chosen Girls to come back?"

We ran back onstage and everyone cheered. For the closing song, we did one Mello and Trin had started together.

Trin sang the first verse:

I pick up the paper and I just can't understand
every single day I see
the chance of peace
just slipping through our hands.
Got to say I hate it every time I turn the page.
It's so complicated.
I feel jaded.
But I hold on to my faith.

Cole took over on the bridge. I closed my eyes and had to remind myself to keep playing bass as his smooth voice sang:

What can I do when I'm hitting the wall?
I wanna think big but I gotta start small.
Cuz it's better doin' something than nothing at all.

I smiled as Trin came back in for a duet on the part of the song I wrote, the chorus:

I'm just one voice —
a whisper in the dark.
I'm just one voice,
but I can do my part.
Cuz if love's what I choose
and if I speak the truth
who knows what one voice can do.

Mello and Karson sang the second bridge together. They sounded way excellent.

And if a million mouths said a million prayers tonight,
and if a million hearts showed the world they care tonight,
we could make it right.

Everyone loved the song. It was a great way to wrap a concert where we really were doing something to make it right.

Mr. Camillo made us wait onstage as he came up to make final announcements. "Congratulations, Hopetown!" he yelled into the mike. "Tonight you donated over one thousand cans of food to our new food pantry. And ticket sales brought in" — he stopped to clear his throat and wipe his eyes — "tickets to tonight's concert brought in $15,420!"

I think we screamed louder than anyone. Over $15,000? As soon as the applause died down, Trin said, "Back tables. Let's go!"

Lamont served as our bodyguard, holding off fans until we got to the back of the room. Cole, Karson, and Hunter helped us pull out DVDs and leftover purses and necklaces. We spread them out on long tables so people could see everything easily. Hunter held up a blue and green necklace and said, "This is actually pretty nice-looking junk."

"*Gracias*," I answered. "I guess."

"Where's my sign?" Mello asked. "I made a sign that listed prices and explained tonight's profits go to the shelter."

I reached the bottom of a box of purses. "Here it is!"

We slapped it on the wall with masking tape and got busy selling stuff, giving autographs, and signing up volunteers to work at the shelter.

My fourth or fifth customer was a young woman with long brown hair. I thought she looked familiar. She held some bills out to me. I took the money and asked, "Did you get a purse, a necklace, or a CD?"

She smiled, and her enormous blue eyes lit up. "I got bananas and grapes."

"Oh!" I said, remembering. "I met you at the grocery store, didn't I?" I looked at the bills in my hand. "And you found your money. I'm glad."

"That's not all I found," she said, leaning over the table toward me. "I got a job!"

"Cool frijoles! Where are you working?" I asked.

"Here," she answered. "I'm the first full-time employee for the new food pantry. The captain even offers day care for employees' kids, so my little ones will be here in the same building. Isn't it perfect?"

I reached across the table and hugged her. "It's beyond perfect. Thanks for telling me."

She shook her head. "No, thank *you*. For the fruit and for the food pantry. You changed everything for me and my kids."

I just had time to wipe a happy tear away before Trin called, "Harmony, someone down here has a few questions about your necklaces."

I got Lamont to take my spot and joined Trin, Mello, and a tall, dark-skinned woman in an olive-colored suit.

The woman held a perfectly manicured hand out to me. "Harmony, my name is Athena Winters, and I am intrigued by the design of your necklaces. How long have you been making jewelry?"

I felt my face grow warm with pleasure. "A few years," I answered.

She held up one of my favorites—a blend of various-colored glass beads and silver crosses. "This is absolutely lovely," she said. "The color combination is fresh and different—it really works."

"Thank you," I answered, not sure what else to say.

"And these purses," she added, picking up a blue one with green trim. "Mello, Trin tells me you design the bags?"

Mello nodded, grinning.

"Fabulous," Athena gushed. "Very elegant, but young and exciting at the same time." She waved her hand over the table. "You three actually make all these products by hand?"

"Yes," Trin answered, flexing her fingers. "I have the pinpricks to prove it."

"How do you find the time?" Athena asked. "Between your music and work here at the shelter, you must stay pretty busy."

We nodded.

"What will you do when school starts?"

"We won't be able to make as much," Trin admitted. "Besides, everything's about to change."

"We just signed a contract with Shining Stars," I explained. "We'll be going on tours all over the world."

Athena said, "Congratulations! I've never heard of Shining Stars, but music is not my line." She looked at the necklaces again and asked, "Have you ever thought about having your lines mass-produced? I know some artists feel like something is lost in mass production. I think it's simply a chance for more people to enjoy what you've created."

"Do you mean, like, getting a factory to make our stuff for us?" Mello asked.

"Right," Athena agreed.

Trin laughed. "We've dreamed about it. But we don't have that kind of money."

"It doesn't always take money," Athena explained. "Actually, if someone from a large, reputable company wanted to pick up your line, they would pay *you* for the right to produce your product. You would also get a percentage of the profit for each item sold. Since your products would be sold all over the country, it would be quite lucrative." She smiled at Trin. "And no more pinpricks." She gathered up four purses and six necklaces. "I would love to see you make a deal like that. First of all, your products are outstanding. Second, I like what you stand for."

She pulled out her wallet and started counting out bills to pay for her stuff.

I said, "Well, if you ever happen to run into someone who works for a place like that, tell them about us."

Trin gave Athena her change, and she tucked it into her wallet. Then she pulled out a small white card and handed it to me.

It said:

Athena Winters
Vice President of Product Development
Ivy Leaf Accessories

I could hardly breathe. I said, "You work for Ivy Leaf?"

"*The* Ivy Leaf?" Trin squealed. "That sells those killer handbags?"

"And gorgeous jewelry?" Mello added, her eyes huge. "In all the fancy stores?"

Athena smiled. "I do," she answered, holding her hand out to me for a handshake. "What do you think? Do you all like the idea of a Chosen Girls line of handbags and jewelry being sold nationwide?"

"A nationwide deal?" I repeated, looking at Trin and Mello. They covered their mouths, but I could still hear their happy squeals. "It looks like a big day for the Chosen Girls."

"A big day? Absolutely," Larinda said, elbowing her way up to the table. "And a long one. It's fifteen after nine, and I have work to do yet. So can we get our meeting under way?"

I looked at Athena apologetically. "She's our new agent," I explained.

She smiled and said, "You have my card. Call me."

I nodded.

Larinda looked around. "I don't suppose this … shelter … has a meeting room we could use?"

"Of course it does," Trin answered. "Guys, can you cover the tables?" The KCH crew nodded, and Trin turned back to Larinda. "Follow me."

We headed for the captain's office. As soon as we got in and shut the door, Larinda claimed the captain's large desk. She popped open her briefcase and started pulling papers out. Then she dropped the first bomb.

"I want to be sure you understand the pace is much faster on the professional track. For instance, I'll need lyrics for five new songs by Friday."

"Five?" Mello exclaimed. "That's a song a day!"

"I'm glad to see you're proficient at math," Larinda said with a smirk. "I hope you're as good at writing. And no more of that religious drivel you've been producing. Fans want songs about boys and parties, not faith and God."

Trin looked like she wanted to strangle her. "What? You can't tell us what to sing!"

Larinda didn't even look at Trin. "Next item of business: costuming," she said, pulling out a sketchbook and handing it to Mello. "You may each choose two outfits from these drawings."

Mello's eyes got huge. "No way am I going onstage in any of these."

I whispered, "Mello, this is not the time to be picky."

She practically threw the drawings at me. "Oh!" I said in dismay. "*No es bueno.* These clothes barely cover any skin! What's the point?"

"The point is, this is what people want to see," Larinda answered.

Trin shook her head. "Look, woman—I mean, Larinda—we have standards."

"Which change as of tonight," Larinda shot back. "From now on your new standard is what will increase your ratings. Bring in the most money."

"That isn't how we function," I argued. "Our band stands for something. There's a reason we perform."

"It's a little late to get worked up about your so-called 'morals,'" Larinda said, making quotation marks in the air. She rapped her fingernails against her copy of the contract. "You signed, remember? It's all in here. So ... I'll leave you to choose your costumes and get working on those lyrics!" She put the contract in her briefcase and clicked across the office floor and out the door.

chapter • 13

•••

Still sunday

As the agent exited, Lamont entered. "Who was that?" he asked, looking behind him.

"Larinda Higgins," Trin wailed.

I shoved the drawings at him. "Look what she wants us to wear!"

"And she wants five new songs by Friday," Mello added. "And they can't be about anything we believe in!"

Lamont held up his hands and said, "Whoa. Since when does a perfect stranger get to tell you what to wear and what to sing about?"

"Since we signed this," I said, holding up our copy of the contract.

Lamont slid into the captain's chair and took the stack of papers. He read the first page and said, "That woman is your new agent?"

We nodded.

He read further. "This says your songs 'will not contain any objectionable content. Objectionable content includes but is not limited to: opinions about God, Jesus, Christianity, faith, and/or any particular belief system. Such opinions could be offensive to those who choose another path or choose not to believe at all.' Did she tell you the contract said that?"

"She said the thing about no objectionable content," Trin answered. "I assumed that meant nasty words or vulgar ideas."

Lamont turned the page. "Here's what it says about clothes: 'Band members will perform only in costumes approved by AGENT.'"

"This is way horrible," Mello said.

"It gets worse," Lamont responded, pointing to another section. "Did she talk to you about the money?"

I nodded. "She told us that's the whole point—making more of it," I explained.

Lamont snorted. "Yeah, I can see why. According to this contract, she gets seventy-five percent of everything the band brings in."

"Seventy-five percent?" Trin asked, getting up. She paced back and forth beside the booth. "So we're wearing skimpy outfits, singing songs about meaningless stuff, and we don't even get to keep the money?"

I felt a hot tear run down my face. "So we can't help people?" I didn't want to look at Trin and Mello, so I stared at my feet. "That's the whole reason we signed. To make a difference in the world. You were right," I whispered. "You were right not to trust me. I've completely killed the Chosen Girls!"

"It's not your fault," Mello said, reaching across for my hand. "Larinda's the one we shouldn't have trusted."

Trin tossed her pink hair in disgust. "Remember what she said? 'If you can't trust me, who can you trust?'"

"Seriously!" Mello said. "I'm going to be afraid to trust anyone after this."

"It's a little late to bring it up," Lamont said, reaching into his pocket and pulling out a leather wallet. "But I know the answer."

"To what?" I asked.

"To Larinda's question about who to trust," he answered. He pulled a dollar bill out and tossed it onto the table.

Trin stopped pacing and looked at the dollar. "Huh?"

Lamont tapped a bony finger on the bill. "This says it all. Put your trust anywhere else, and you'll be disappointed every time."

"Money?" I bellowed. "You are so wrong, Lamont. I *did* trust money — that if we made enough of it, we could save the world. It didn't work, Lamont. And let me tell you, I'm way disappointed."

"You're missing my point, Harmony. Or maybe you're making my point for me," Lamont said, sitting back and crossing his arms. "Pick up that dollar. What does it say?"

I picked up the bill. "Federal reserve note. The United States of America," I read.

"Turn it over," Lamont instructed.

I flipped it over and read, "The United States of America." Then I said, "Oh." I looked at Lamont and felt a weak smile tug at one corner of my mouth.

"Read it out loud, Harmony."

I sighed. "In God we trust."

He nodded. "Now we're getting somewhere. Have you women ever read Proverbs 3, verses five and six?"

"Of course," Trin answered, crossing her arms. "I memo-rized it, like, a hundred years ago. 'Trust in the Lord with all your heart and lean not on your own understanding; in all your ways acknowledge him, and he will make your paths straight.'"

"Beautiful," Lamont said. "Only one thing more powerful than memorizing scripture." He sat nodding to himself.

Trin, Mello, and I looked at each other, waiting for him to go on.

Mello caved first. "OK, Lamont, and what is that?"

He smiled. "Glad you asked. I'd say the only thing more powerful than learning the Bible is applying it to your life. Ever thought about trying that?"

I slapped my palms down on the desk. "Wait a minute, Lamont. I think you've forgotten who you're talking to. We're the Chosen Girls, remember? Chosen by God to make a dif-ference. We know about applying the Bible to our lives, OK? Did you listen tonight? We sing songs about trusting God."

"Excuse me," he said, sliding out from behind the desk. "I thought you were the women who just signed a contract promising to wear sleazy clothes, sing songs about partying, and give all your money to a corrupt agent who'll spend it on who knows what." He started for the office door.

"Lamont!" Trin called. "Come back. You're right. We didn't live by the Bible. We sing about it, but we don't always do it."

Mello sighed. "We didn't acknowledge God," she agreed. "We didn't pray about the agent at all. We decided to sign because it seemed like a good idea—"

"Based on your *own understanding*," Lamont finished for her. He looked up, like he could see God right there in the office. "God wants to make your path straight, but he won't force you to do things his way."

"I wish he would," I admitted. "We've gotten ourselves into a serious mess."

Trin asked, "Do you think it's too late to ask him to get us out of it?"

Lamont held his hands out to Trin and me. We grabbed them and reached for Mello's. "It's never too late to turn to God," he answered.

After we prayed, we all went to Lamont's house. He got on the Internet and searched while we paced his media room and prayed some more.

"This just keeps getting worse," Lamont said, shaking his head. "Mmm, mmm, you sure got yourselves in a heap of trouble."

"What? What is it? Quit moaning and tell us something," I demanded.

"It looks like your Miss Larinda *is* the Shining Stars Agency. She's solo, and she doesn't have a great rep."

"No way," Mello said. "She told Harmony the agency is in New York. It's huge."

"Yeah. Shining Stars represents the biggest names in pop, rock, and country," Trin added.

"Nope," Lamont said, leaning back and crossing his arms. "Looks like it's just her and her big mouth. She's already been reported to the Better Business Bureau for trying to make fraudulent deals. Didn't you guys check out any of her claims?"

Trin said, "I told Harmony to get references."

"I told her to get a list of bands," Mello added.

"I blew it," I admitted. "Big-time."

Lamont shook his head again and went back to typing. I jumped when he yelled, "Oh, happy day! Here it is." His smile seemed to light up the room as he pointed to the monitor. "Any contract with a minor is void. The minor has the option to terminate the contract in the absence of an adult cosigner."

"What does that mean?" Trin asked.

"It means God provided a way out. You're all minors—none of you are eighteen or older. You don't have to stick with the terms of the contract, because the contract is no good!"

"But why didn't Larinda know about that law?" Mello asked.

I said, "Maybe she isn't the brightest bulb on the Christmas tree."

"So can we send her an email right now?" Trin asked, rubbing her hands together. "I can't wait to tell her we'll sing about God all we want."

"And wear outfits *we* pick out," Mello added.

"And use the money we make to help people," I said. I couldn't help but sigh. "Even though it won't be much."

"Don't forget the possibilities with Ivy Leaf," Trin reminded us.

"Right!" I agreed.

Lamont pulled up his email. "I'm ready. Tell me what to type."

Trin said, " 'Dear Larinda.' "

"Dear?" Mello asked. "I wouldn't call her dear. More like Horrible Larinda."

I said, "No. Too hateful. Maybe something like Conniving Larinda?"

Lamont erased *Dear* and left just *Larinda*.

"Good enough," Trin told him. "Now say, 'We regret to inform you that we plan to terminate our contract with you.' "

"Regret?" Mello asked. "We don't regret it. We're totally psyched to terminate it."

"We're psyched to terminate it, but we aren't psyched about informing her," I corrected. "At least I'm not. She's going to freak."

"True," Trin agreed. "Besides, it would be seriously rude to write and say, 'Evil Larinda, we're so pumped to dump you!'"

"I can see that," Mello conceded. "Fun, but rude."

"As we are all considered minors under the law, and no adult cosigners were present," Trin continued, "the contract we signed is null and void."

"Ooh!" I said. "Null and void. Go, Trin! You sound like a lawyer." She bonked fists with me and concluded with, "Sincerely, the Chosen Girls."

I gave Lamont Larinda's address, and he typed it in and hit Send.

"We're free. I feel like celebrating!" I said, hugging Mello and Trin.

Mello smiled and held up the contract. "We won't need this anymore. Let's use it to make confetti!"

We each took a few sheets of that awful document and ripped them into tiny pieces. Trin led us in a prayer of thanks to God, and then we yelled, "Chosen Girls rock!" We threw the paper into the air and laughed as it floated down all over us.

"Awesome," Lamont said. He looked at the white bits all over the carpet. "Now you can help me clean it up."

"First, I need to send an email to Makayla," I told him.

Trin and Mello both said, "Makayla? You're still talking to her?"

"It's almost eleven, and practice for the Makayla Simmons band starts early tomorrow," I explained. "I need to let her know I'm going to be late."

I watched their jaws drop before I added, "Very, very late. As in—I'm never going to show up to be in her band."

Mello laughed. "Now *that* sounds like an email that will be fun to write!"

CHECK OUT this excerpt from book six in the Chosen Girls series.

SOLD OUT

kidz

Created & Illustrated by G Studios
Written by Cheryl Crouch

chapter · 1

· · ·

I can't believe how fast Mello and Harmony became my best-ever friends after I moved to California. Of course, starting our own band definitely helped. The Chosen Girls have had so many crazy experiences together—that stuff makes for way serious bonding.

It's cool because it feels like I've known them forever, instead of just a year. Sometimes I wish they knew me as well as I know them, and sometimes I'm glad they don't. I mean, they know me. They just don't know everything about me. Like, that my family isn't the perfect family they think we are. It's not like my friends couldn't handle the truth—maybe I'm the one who can't deal.

· · ·

I leaned across the cafeteria table and asked, "So we're meeting at the tryouts, right?"

"*Sí*," Harmony answered. "Four thirty. That should give us time to warm up."

Mello tapped the edge of the table. "I wonder how many bands will show."

Jasmine, a friend from church sitting at the next table, turned around and said, "Couldn't help overhearing. What are you trying out for?"

"Pizza Pete's wants a band for their new ad campaign," I explained.

Jasmine looked starstruck. "That is so awesome. Do you Chosen Girls even *know* how cool you are?"

"We have a pretty good idea," Harmony said, grinning then ducking to avoid the wadded-up napkin Mello chucked at her.

"So will the ads, like, be on TV?" Jasmine asked.

Makayla's voice came from behind me. "Yes, they'll be on TV, and the Makayla Simmons band can't wait to star in them."

I saw Makayla, the self-appointed leader of the Snob Mob, standing between tables with a tiny girl I didn't recognize.

"So you're trying out too?" I asked, forcing my mouth into a smile.

Makayla flung her short silvery-blonde hair. "A formality. I don't know why *anyone else* should bother showing up."

"Are you the Chosen Girls?" asked the girl with Makayla.

I said, "Yeah, hi. What's your name?"

The petite girl grinned shyly and said, "I'm Reesie." Even though her hair and eyes were still the same mousy brown, her whole face seemed to glow when she smiled.

Makayla huffed in obvious disgust. "Reesie, this is Harmonica," she said with a shrug in Harmony's direction. "That's Melodious, and you're speaking to Trendy."

"That's what Makayla calls us," I said. "The rest of the world knows us as Harmony, Mello, and Trin. Are you new at James Moore?"

She nodded. "New to California too. Just moved here from Oregon."

"You'll love it," Mello offered. "There's so much to —"

Makayla held onto her empty lunch tray with one hand and grabbed Reesie's elbow with the other. "Yeah, well, she's not looking for things to do or for new friends. But since she's my new bass player, it's probably good she met the 'other' band. Not that you're any *real* competition."

I bit my lip to keep from pointing out how many times our band has left hers in the dust. It didn't matter, because Harmony blurted, "Unless you count the channel 34 contest and the Hopetown Battle of the —"

"Yeah, let's talk about the Battle of the Bands," Makayla agreed. "The *L.A.* Battle of the Bands."

Harmony rolled her eyes in frustration.

I whispered, "It's just Makayla, Harmony. Let it go."

Reesie pulled away from Makayla and asked, "Which of you plays bass?"

Harmony lifted her hand. "I do."

"I hear you're fantastic," Reesie offered. "Maybe we could jam sometime."

Makayla snorted. "I'm sure Harmony could learn a thing or two from you, Reesie. She's got plenty of room for improvement."

"You must not think she's too bad, since you begged her to join *your* band," I reminded Makayla.

Reesie completely ignored our exchange. "So what else are you into?"

Harmony pretended to snap a picture. "I'm a photographer for the yearbook. And I make jewelry." She jangled the bracelet on her wrist.

"She's also a blue belt in karate," Mello added proudly.

Makayla put her hand to her face. "Ooh! I'm so scared."

Reesie nodded. "Cool. What about you, Mello?"

Mello shrugged. "I'm the drummer. And I do layouts for the yearbook."

"She designs purses too," I said, holding up the one Mello made just for me.

"That's hideous," Makayla said, wrinkling her pug nose. "It's the exact same shade of pink as your hair."

Reesie reached out to touch the satiny fabric. "I love it. How do I get one?"

Harmony whipped out one of our little business cards. She handed it to Reesie as the bell rang, and everyone started picking up trays and filling the aisles. I stood up and grabbed mine.

"I didn't get to find out much about you, Trin," Reesie apologized. "Maybe next time. Right now, Makayla's going to show me where my next class is."

"There's nothing to know about Trin," Makayla told her as they inched toward the tray return. Even though she faced away from me, I could hear Makayla's voice clearly.

"I don't know why Trin acts like she's so great," Makayla continued. "If Harmony and Mello hadn't felt sorry for her and taken her in when she moved here, she'd be an absolute nobody. She's just a new girl who sings in the Chosen Girls, and that's it. Except for the band, she's a nobody."

I slammed my tray back onto the table. "The new girl?" I yelled. "A nobody? I've been here a whole year!"

Mello and Harmony looked at each other like, *Uh-oh.*

"Is that what people at this school think of me? That I'm the new girl who sings for Chosen Girls and *that's it*?"

Harmony leaned across the table. "It's just Makayla, Trin. Let it go."

"Did you guys really feel sorry for me?" I asked, dropping back into my seat as Makayla's words sunk in. "Is that why you're my friends?"

"Right, Trin," Mello answered. "There's something about you that brings out our natural feelings of pity. Maybe it's the fact that you're drop-dead gorgeous and always dressed like a runway model."

"Or it could be your outgoing personality," Harmony added.

Mello grinned. "No, I think it's your amazing voice and the way you make an electric guitar sing. Poor Trin."

"You're so pitiful we had to force ourselves to take you in," Harmony finished. She reached across the table to give my shoulder a squeeze, then she and Mello picked up their stuff and joined the crowd waiting to turn in trays. I made myself follow them, but I didn't join in their conversation about Reesie and how someone so nice could have ended up in Makayla's band.

As I put my tray on the conveyor belt and watched it disappear, I thought, *What if everyone in the school thinks like Makayla? There is more to me than singing in our band. The time has come for me to show the people of James Moore what I'm made of.*

••

That afternoon, I sat in science, trying to listen but unable to stop thinking about Makayla and what I could do to prove myself to her—something that would show the whole school who I am.

When my phone vibrated in my pocket, I clicked into my inbox to find the text message:

Hi, honey. Sorry it's been so long since I've written. I may be in your area two weeks from now, and I'd like to come see you if I can work it out. Love, Jake

As soon as I saw his name, I felt that same mixed-up feeling I get every time he decides to write. Excited, angry, hopeful … sad. How can one person make me feel all that?

I guess that's the power a father has. Especially one who walks out on you when you're just four years old.

I didn't reply to his message in class. I knew better than to try that. Mrs. Lewis would take up my phone in a flash. I didn't want to end up explaining to everybody in science about Jake. I hadn't even told Harmony and Mello about Mom's divorce and that my biological father lived in Colorado. It didn't seem necessary, since my mom's new husband, Jeff Adams, adopted me when I turned seven. For all anyone in Hopetown knew, we were a perfect family.

My real father's leaving was ancient history and had nothing to do with my life now.

Besides, for some stupid reason, his messages usually make me cry.

So I spent the rest of class worrying about Jake's text message *and* what Makayla said. I didn't learn a thing about the periodic table. Just a bunch of letters and numbers up there on the wall.

When the bell rang I rushed to a bathroom stall. I stood there and held my phone for a while, trying to convince myself I didn't care what Jake had to say. So he was my "real" dad. So, even now, I could remember each word of the goofy lullaby he sang to me every night. And the spicy smell of his aftershave when I kissed him good-bye every morning.

Until that one morning, when I woke up and he wasn't there.

Did those memories give him the right to barge in on my life when I hadn't heard from him for two years?

I'd like to come see you.

Did he mean it? He always promised to come, but he never showed.

What if he really came this time? Would it be good or bad for him to visit me in Hopetown?

I left the bathroom and pushed through the crowded hall. I thought about my friends he'd never met and events we'd won that he didn't know about. Would he be impressed with my life here? What would he think of California? Of the Chosen Girls?

More important, what would my father think of me?

• • •

I sat by my friend Latisha Punch during math. Latisha started talking about her work for student council the minute the bell rang for the end of class.

"They gave me the talent show this year!"

"Ohwow!" I answered as I gathered up my books. "Latisha, that's awesome."

She widened her brown eyes in horror. "Hello, girlfriend?" she said. "You might as well carry a sign that says, 'Kick me. I'm new.'"

"Huh?" I asked. "What do you mean?"

She rolled her eyes as we headed into the crowded hall. "The talent show at James Moore is famous, Trin. Famous for being way, way beyond lame. It stinks. It's stupid and boring, and nobody who's anybody wants to come within a hundred yards of it. Weren't you here during last year's talent show?"

"I don't remember hearing about one," I answered.

She nodded. "There ya go."

"It can't be that bad," I insisted.

"The winner did a juggling act."

I thought about it. "Juggling can be cool."

Latisha shook her head. "Not when the person is only juggling two balls. And still manages to miss half the time."

I laughed out loud. "You're kidding. That was the winning act?"

"It's not funny," she said, maneuvering us around a group of chatting cheerleaders. "The runner-up played a solo. You know that old song 'You Light Up My Life'?"

"Sure," I answered with a giggle. "It's a classic."

"Well, it doesn't sound so classic when it's played on the kazoo. I'm telling you, the show reeks."

"But Latisha, if you're in charge, you can change all that," I told her. "Wouldn't it be fun to make it a huge success?"

"And just how do you suggest I do that?" she asked, as we stopped outside her next class. "And don't say, 'By letting the Chosen Girls be in it.' It's strictly amateur."

"Wait," I said, leaning against the door frame. "When is it?"

"In just two weeks," she answered with a groan.

"What if my band did a grand finale kind of thing? Like while the judges tally the scores."

Her face lit up. "Would you really? You'd do that for me? Don't say it if you don't mean it. Because, Trin, I'm telling you, I think if a big-name band like yours got involved, it might get other people interested. Maybe we could even get on the news or something!"

The warning bell rang. "I've gotta go," I said. "But count on the Chosen Girls. And count on me too."

"Thanks, Trin," she yelled after me. "I'm so stoked. You're saving me from social suicide. Finally, it won't just be the nobody show."

As I rushed down the hall, Latisha's words echoed in my head. Maybe I could help her out and help myself at the same time. I knew I could make the talent show off-the-charts amazing.

Then Makayla will know I'm not a nobody, I thought. *I won't be "the new girl who's in Chosen Girls." I'll be Trin Adams, whose leadership skills transformed the show — and the whole school — into something to be proud of.*

And if my real father happens to visit during the talent show and get blown away by the way-fabulous job his daughter did on it, well, that won't hurt, either.

Chosen Girls is a dynamic new series that communicates a message of empowerment and hope to Christian youth who want to live out their faith. These courageous and compelling girls stand for their beliefs and encourage others to do the same. When their cross-cultural outreach band takes off, Trinity, Melody, and Harmony explode onto the scene with style, hot music, and genuine, age-relatable content.

Backstage Pass

Book One • Softcover • ISBN O-31O-71267-X

In *Backstage Pass*, shy, reserved Melody gets her world rocked when a new girl moves in across the street from her best friend, Harmony. Soon downtime—or any time with Harmony at all—looks like a thing of the past as the strong-willed Trinity invades Melody and Harmony's world and insists that the three start a rock band.

Available now at your local bookstore!

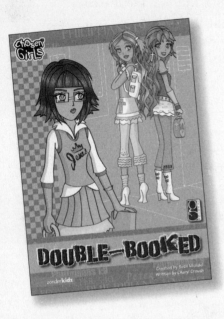

Double-Booked

Book Two • Softcover • ISBN O-31O-71268-8

In *Double-Booked*, Harmony finds
that a three-way friendship is challenging,
with Trinity befriending a snobby clique
and Melody all negative. Through a
series of mistakes, Harmony unwittingly
unites the two against her and learns that
innocent comments hurt more than you
think. Ultimately, the Chosen Girls
are united again in time to sing for
a crowd that really needs to hear
what they have to say.

Unplugged

Book Three • Softcover • ISBN O-31O-71269-6

The band lands a fantastic opportunity
to travel to Russia, but the "international
tour," as they dub it, brings out Trinity's
take-charge personality. Almost
too confidently, she tries to control
fundraising efforts and the tour to avoid
another mess by Harmony. But cultural
challenges, band member clashes, and
some messes of her own convince
Trinity she's not really in charge after all.
God is. And his plan includes changed
lives, deepened faith, and improved
relationships with her mom and friends.

Available now at your local bookstore!

Solo Act

Book Four • Softcover • ISBN O-31O-7127O-X

Melody needs some downtime—and the summer youth retreat will really hit the spot! But a last-minute crisis at camp means an opportunity for the band to lead worship every morning, plus headline the camp's big beach concert and go to camp for free. Too busy and unhappy, Melody makes some selfish choices that result in the girls getting lost, sunburned, in trouble, and embarrassed. Can she pull out of the downward spiral before she ruins camp—and the band—completely?

Sold Out

Book Six • Softcover • ISBN O-31O-71272-6

Dedicated to proving herself to others, Trinity gets involved in organizing the school talent show. Before she knows it, she accepts a dare from Chosen Girls' rival band to be decided by the outcome of a commercial audition.

Overload

Book Seven • Softcover • ISBN 0-310-71273-4

Melody discovers a latent talent for leadership that she never knew
she had. When she begins a grief recovery group for kids like her,
she loses her focus on the work God is doing
through the Chosen Girls.

Available now at your local bookstore!

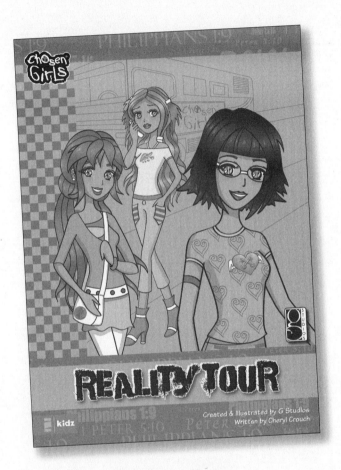

Reality Tour

Book Eight • Softcover • ISBN 0-310-71274-2

When the Chosen Girls go on their first multi-city tour in a borrowed RV, Harmony's messiness almost spoils their final show. What's worse, she almost blows her opportunity to witness to her cousin Lucinda.

We want to hear from you. Please send your comments
about this book to us in care of zreview@zondervan.com. Thank you.